BECOMING DAD

25 Stories About Everything

Casey Freeland

for Leslie who will think this shouldn't be for her

Becoming Dad

CONTENTS

Becoming Dad

CONTENTS *(cont.)*

Becoming Dad

CHAPTER ONE – BECOMING DAD

I read Tuesday's With Morrie about two years ago, the Mitch Albom story that follows a man's experiences each Tuesday with an older man who is going to die. It's a short creation, much like this, but the book stuck to me and forced me to look at my life and that of my father's and how one created the other. Mitch, thank you for that, you son of a bitch. Like I didn't have enough to think about.

Once upon a time a man named Howard Lee Freeland graced this planet with his spirit. Had the planet known what it was in for, the tumble he took out of the rumble seat of a model "T" Ford as a teen would have killed him, certainly, because this ball of dirt has never been the same.

Born on December 11th, 1922 to a man named Victor - a twin to Verner H. Where the H didn't stand for anything but H - in Alameda, California, Howard would find it in his short life to outlast two wives and create eight children. Six of those children created nineteen grandchildren. Two (twins again) didn't make it past the first few weeks of life. Only one pair of twins among the grands, which I consider a bit of a failure with the ratios we had working for us. We should have done much better.

At any rate (one of his favorite things to say) Howard served in WWII, as did many, fought snipers in the steamy jungles of Burma after being trained to battle on snow skis in Colorado, and returned with an appreciation for life. He became a salesman, although that would be a bit like becoming Irish (see Chapter 3) and proceeded to procreate.

This story is not about my father, at least not in a biographical sense, which may or may not please my four sisters, especially sister number two. I only say that because she is my internal editor. That's correct, I actually hear her voice when I'm editing my work. And while reading this, she just found that out. My brother will smile, though, so what the hell.

We begin, you and I, at a campground off Highway 299 East at about three thousand feet in 1973.

A five-year old boy watched the cold, wide creek flow by, the sun glittering off the water, the young mind imagining the fish below, rainbow trout, darting in and out seeking a bit of bug for their afternoon snack. The scent of pine trees, mixed with the baby-powder dust along the trail, filled his nostrils. He squatted and patted the dirt with his hand, watching the clouds puff up and out, caught also by the brightness of the day. He tasted the dirt on his teeth and tongue and felt it against his cheek, on his knees, between the toes of his bare feet.

Another aroma found him and tugged at his stomach. He stood and ran back to the concrete barbecue that threw hot-dog-filled smoke into the air like Indian signals of lunch. He reached up and grabbed the barbecue-flavored chips from the red-painted picnic table - the one with the P & C 4-ever and John P wuz here carved across the seat - and had a mouthful of the greasy delicacy before anyone could force him to wash his hands.

His brother - not yet a brother but rather a smelly, wet mess of a baby who took attention away from all who adored the boy - watched the chips go into the boy's mouth from his seat atop the table. The boy stuck out a tongue covered with half-chewed food. The wet mess smiled. The boy flicked wet mess' big toe as hard as he could, but it only tickled and made him giggle. He looked across the table and grabbed a long, wooden spoon, rearing back for a good, solid smack against wet mess' fat leg. Someone, one of the many adults watching over the boy, snatched it away and gave him a stern look and a finger shake. Sister number three, twenty-one years old and already making her own wet messes.

"Go wash up," she said. "The dogs are almost ready."

"Awwwwww," the boy complained.

"Now!"

The boy walked over to the pump, gave it a few giant pulls, and put his hands under the faucet. A breath later, a gush of icy water spilled out, splashing to the ground and rinsing the salty sweetness and most of the dirt from his tiny fingers.

The boy never got to eat his hot dog.

When he turned back to the camp site, the adults had gathered in a tight group near sister number two, who must have just arrived because the boy didn't remember seeing her there at all. They all had their arms around each other like a football huddle. The boy stood and watched them, straining to hear their whispers. His feet felt cold from the pump's overzealous gush, now mixing with the dirt and pine needles strewn across the ground. The birds overhead - once singing loud and harshly as if trying to overcome the babbling of the creek - stopped as if they waited with the boy.

After much more time than the young boy's mind could count, they turned towards him, all of them, and he saw tears in their eyes and heavy, open-mouthed frowns on their faces, and he became afraid.

His closest sister, sister number four, just back from the bathroom shack across the campground, bounded up beside the boy and pushed him. He lost his footing and nearly toppled over, which she did not want. She steadied him, panting and smiling her big-toothed smile, and then followed his brown eyes with her blue to the group of grown ups standing together.

"Mommy?" she said, her face dropping, her grip on the boy's arm abruptly and painfully tight.

"She's not here," the boy said.

Sister number two, the strongest of the sisters, detached from the adults, approached the boy and girl and knelt in front of them, facing them eye-to-eye. To the boy her tears looked like a giant's tears, like the gushing of the pump had splashed on her face when the boy washed his hands. He felt guilty for it as if he was the cause of the sad adults.

"There's been an accident," she said, her voice shaky and deep.

The boy looked up at sister number four and saw tears cascading down her face as well.

"Your Mom has been in an accident," she said. "Uh, her car. On her way to work this morning, there was an accident."

"Mommy?" sister number four said again as if she had forgotten all other words.

"I'm sorry, sweetheart. She didn't make it. Mommy can't come home."

The boy's little world literally spun. The trees and dirt, the pump and red picnic table, the talking creek and now silent Jays, the adults standing and staring stupidly back at him, sister number four and sister number two, it all spun, turning on an axis as fast as a top, tumbling around him and falling away.

A cloud formed around the boy, a fog laying thick against his skin, cold in the warm Spring afternoon, misting away the campground and the people whom he loved, but not as much as Mommy. Now and again a hand would take him and lead him here or there. Now and again a voice would tell him to brush his teeth or wash his face, neither of which he did. Now and again another child would look at him and he knew they had talked about him, about the kid who didn't have a mom. Strange adults would stare at him with pitied expressions he hated. And time ate away days upon days of the boy's life, as his little mind worked.

His mind worked and succeeded, eventually, in bringing the boy back out of the mist and into the world. Later, the boy would not know if it took days or months, but slowly the fog blew away and the sun became bright again and there were smiles and jokes and fun.

People still mentioned the day and said they were sorry. The boy never knew what to say. He tried thank you but he wasn't thankful at all. He said that it was okay a few times, but he knew it wasn't. Finally he settled on silence, and mostly people stopped saying it, which suited him.

He finished kindergarten, had his first kiss, went to Disneyland and played through a summer of garden hoses, bugs and wrestling with sister number four. He picked on his little brother, who no longer seemed a wet mess, but rather a loud, screaming fit. He threw rocks and made mud and pulled grass from the lawn and leaves from the trees. He ate strawberries and watermelon and drank root beer that made him burp long and loud. He enjoyed dozens of hot dogs and handfuls of his favorite barbecue potato chips.

And he forgot.

The boy's mind worked and worked all through those first months after his mom was thrown from her car after plummeting down a steep embankment, a cliff really, and slammed her head against a rock that killed her instantly. The boy's mind labored against itself for survival so that the boy could still be a boy and not be taken somewhere else.

By the time the boy started first grade, his school across the street from the cemetery where they had put his mother's body in the ground, he had forgotten her almost completely. And he hadn't cried a single tear.

CHAPTER TWO – THE MORE THE MERRIER

Still with me? Amazing. I know, I know. What a terrible thing to write. I can't apologize for this book though, or it won't ever be written. Despite chapter one, this is not a gloom-and-doom, woe-is-me read. But I had to start at the beginning, and for me that was the beginning. "You mean it's true?" you ask. "True is such a strange little four letter word," I reply. "Well either it's true or it isn't," you retort. "Not so, not so," I chide. "Truth is as varied as each individual human being, distorted and contorted by each person's beliefs, experiences, intelligence, wisdom, loves, hates and virtually everything else. When you look at how different we all are, it is possibly the biggest miracle of life that we can get along at all." You don't reply because you are now asleep. We should get on with the story.

I believe I've mentioned that my father had a lot of children. And those children had a lot of children. We are not Mormon or Catholic, but we are Irish (see chapter 3.) Here's a fairy tale to chew on while we go forth and multiply.

Dawn broke suddenly across the dry, barren expanse, the mild, rolling hills like giant goose flesh on the arm of the Earth. A structure sat atop one of the unexceptional hills, seen easily from nearly a mile as a speck, not because of its size, for it was small, but because it was the only variance for a thousand miles. At five hundred yards, the home's slanted roof defined its blackness against the brilliant whiteness of the mid-morning sky. At two hundred yards, a ring of greenery appeared like a wreath around the home and the building's gray walls revealed darkened windows and a great silver door. A round, perfect tree grew in front of the home, producing a dark pink fruit shaped like a perfect tear. And at fifty yards, the light breeze carried the sweet chitter of the tiny purple birds living in the tree.

The man opened his eyes and stretched, yawning and growling at the morning. As a night of dreams quickly faded, he looked about the sparse room.

"Hello?" he called. "Love, are you about?"

"Love is not about, sir. Love is exactly where she would be at this time of day, especially today." The manufactured voice spoke with calm emotion and patronized slightly. The voice was the man's creation and specialty.

"I don't like it when you call her Love," he said. "Please reprogram yourself."

"Make me," the voice said.

"Be good." The man rose from the pile of pillows and blankets crumpled on the soft, white floor.

"All right, then. I'll reprogram if you clean your teeth. I can smell you from here."

"A bargain. How about some music to start this momentous day with bliss."

The music was bright and airy and full of strings and flutes and the man hummed along as he pulled his white robe over his dark, naked body. After a toilet and a thorough teeth cleaning, the man thanked the voice and exited out the back of the home through a tinted, glass tube and into the lab.

Like mirrors, the lab's four alabaster walls reflected a ceiling of fierce lights, contrasted against the dull, black floor. An array of monitors flashed and stuttered against the far walls, underscored by panels of keys and switches. A glass cylinder, about ten feet across, rose from floor to ceiling in the center of the room. Within the case sat a gray chair and on the chair, perched with bare feet on the padded seat, bare back to the man, was the woman dressed only in white satin shorts. She was hunched over the back of the chair working with two narrow, pointed tools over a triangular panel of lights inside the chair's back. Her crimson hair trailed straight down her back, far enough to brush the chair as she bobbed back and forth, studying and programming and switching and testing.

"If you're going to dress that way, Love, we'll have to go right here."

She didn't turn, but he heard her smile.

"I believe last night qualifies as an appropriate goodbye, John. I can hardly walk. You animal."

John tried a purr, but had never mastered the rolling tongue.

"Will you miss me?" he asked?

"Of course, Hon, of course." She looked over her bare shoulder at him, offering a buck-toothed smile, her bright blue eyes sparkling under the ceiling lights, which were more than lights, constantly scrubbing the environment, burning air-born particles and cooking unnecessary bacteria.

"Hockey. I can hear it in your voice. You're so excited you can hardly breathe you little tramp. I'm just glad you get the long and I get the short or I would be suicidal."

"Just a week for you, Hon."

"And a year for you, Love."

"Three hundred and fifty seven is all. Just shy."

She jumped off the chair, squeezed through the glass door on the glass cylinder and wrapped her arms tight around John's neck.

"I'll miss you, Hon," she said, her voice shaking and weak. He hugged her back, her body feeling too frail to survive the task at hand. He'd go for her, of course, if she'd let him, which she wouldn't. He'd go with her, of course, if the machine could manage, which it couldn't. So he held her until she pushed him away.

She looked up at him, her eyes so bright they seemed beams of bright blue sunshine.

They made love again, after all, before lunch.

After lunch the woman dressed in simple gray slacks and a simple gray shirt, soft, white shoes with ties over the top in the ancient fashion and a warm, black jacket. Hidden within her jacket were several gadgets that would protect and sustain and a holographic picture of John that would respond kindly to her no matter what she said. By the time they reached the lab again, she had a mild case of hyperventilation. Her hands tremored like the wings of the birds fluttering outside. But when he checked her eyes, they were brave and coherent and he knew she would never postpone the trip.

"I'll be just down the way a bit, Hon," she said easing into the chair as if she had never seen it, as if she hadn't spent the last four years building it, coaxing it into reality.

"Three thousand years."

"A hop and a skip really." John leaned down and kissed her hard, wanting to bruise her already swollen lips so she would remember him more. She kissed him back with the same ferocity, her tongue tasting him as a final goodbye.

Then he closed the glass door in the glass cylinder and walked to the wall with the switches and dials and screen. With one hand on a large green button he looked to her for the go.

She nodded, almost imperceptibly, and he pushed the button, watching his mate vanish in a cloud of wet vapor and flash of purple light.

The week prior to her departure took all of thirty seconds, John following her around, touching her, smelling her, loving her whenever he could pull her away from her project. He knew he annoyed her but didn't much care. He took countless photos of her while working, bathing and cleaning. His favorite shots were when she slept, absolute peace on her face, no brow furrowed with thought, no nervous nibble on her lower lip. He strained to soak up all of her so that her absence would seem trifle, though he knew it wouldn't be.

The week after she left took a lifetime. He could not sleep at all, so every hour was eternal, every minute felt and accounted and marked off the great calendar in his head. The voice spoke to him often, trying to help as he had been programmed. It played the happiest music in its endless library and showed images of the shots he took of her in whatever room he occupied. At night when John couldn't sleep, it sang softly to him the lullabies of another time. After a day or two John told the voice to stop, saying he wanted to feel the loss of her, that he wanted to know this in case anything happened to stop her return.

"If she were to fail on her return I would never forgive myself for any moment of happiness before I knew that to be a fact," John said simply. So the voice stopped, for the most part. It stilled hummed to him when he did sleep, hoping to extend his time of rest.

He moved his blankets and pillows onto the cold floor of the lab the final night, not wanting to miss a second of her return.

Just before sunrise John jerked awake, his head up, his eyes staring into the predawn darkness at the cylinder reflecting dimly the low-lights emanating from the control panels across the room. Something had woken him, he thought, but the room was absolutely still. As he put his head back to the pillow, the room filled with purple light and a howling scream as if the metal beams of the lab's construction were being torn apart.

He covered his ears and blinked against the fiery radiance of the strange light.

In a blink the room returned to near darkness, a damp haze billowing from the glass cylinder.

"Lights," he whispered.

The room lit to its full intensity, instantly drying the vapor that surrounded the chair.

"John?" her voice sought him.

He jumped up and ran to her and lifted her and hugged her tightly.

"Oh, John, it's so good to feel you again."

He set her down and held her hands and looked at his love. She had cut her hair - which he warned her might happen if the style of the time required - to a short bob. Her slacks were a blue, thick fabric adorned with tiny copper-colored buttons, sitting low on her hips and exposing her beautiful stomach. Her top was now a thin fabric adorned with blues and greens and pinks of several different hues, held up by two thin straps over her shoulders. On her feet were sandals of a sort, just a bottom actually with a strap attached at the gap between her first two toes. She was different, older; some of the light in her eyes burned away over the year perhaps, but just as beautiful and just as much his love.

Later that night, as they sat together, cross-legged in their main room on the floor, and he listened to her adventure, and the people and places and machines and entertainments and sounds and horrors and wonders, he was struck dumb by the expanse of it all.

"So they decided to overpopulate?" he asked for the second time.

"I'm telling you John, they made the decision to put as many people on the planet as possible."

"They did it to themselves," he marveled.

"Absolutely. Families were huge. Not three or four, but sometimes six or seven or eight in one home. It was so loud, John. You wouldn't believe the noise. They actually had a name for it. I heard it over and over again. 'The more the merrier.'"

"The chaos of it all must have been maddening for you," John said hopefully.

She became thoughtful, studying the floor.

"At first it was John. At first. But now, here."

"What is it?" But he knew what it was.

She looked at him then, her light blue eyes full of love and hope and purpose.

"Tomorrow I start building," she said.

"What, Love."

She laughed and kissed him hard on the lips.

"A bicycle built for two."

CHAPTER THREE – WE'RE IRISH

Well, that was interesting, some of my sisters may say. My brother will smile when he reads it. He just thinks I'm cool, so whatever I do he tends to give me the benefit of his own optimism. It comes from being five years my junior and I like it just fine.

Now, on to number three, the chapter in which we will explore the finer details of being Irish. I was in my twenties when my sister dug into our genealogy and found our heritage. Before that, I was simply told I was Irish, along with Welsh, English and Dutch. But I liked the Irish bit the most because I was born the day after Saint Patrick's Day and my father named me Casey, my closest sister Kelly and my little brother Carey. Even our dog was named Patty. I remember telling boyhood friends I was half-Irish. As I grew older the ratio became smaller, first a quarter, then an eighth and finally I settled on a sixteenth. But there was still Irish in me, by God. And my sweet little Irish father died knowing his blood ran green. But the joke of it all is our family does not have a single stitch of Irish in it. So the question is, if I believe it long enough, over half my life, doesn't that make me at least a little bit Irish? Can't we just pretend it does?

Here's a story.

The boy was only seven, but he knew a leprechaun when he saw one.

From his first waking moments the boy knew that something special waited on the horizon. The morning sang in cool and sweet and promised something miraculous. He dressed quickly in his

20

grubbies and ran down the narrow steps leading to the first floor of his parents' home. His bare feet slapped against the hardwood floors as he trotted up to the small dining table in the kitchen, already smelling the pancakes and heated syrup.

His father had eaten and sat with paper and pipe. He examined each page like a doctor going over an x-ray, looking for the important parts and making sure the world wasn't broken that day. He sucked wetly on the tobacco filled, mahogany styled pipe between his teeth, steam from his giant cup of coffee mixing with the puffs of smoke. The boy loved the smell of his father, which not coincidentally was the combined aroma of whiskey tobacco, strong black coffee with a mountain of honey, Old Spice Cologne and chewable vitamin C.

The other plates of pancake guts told the boy his two siblings were long gone, already at the helm of their adventures for the day. That was okay with the boy because he didn't feel magic could happen in the midst of non-believers like his brother and sister. He felt magic only happened when a boy could remove himself from everyone else, everyone except the birds and the creatures and the trees.

The boy's mom put a plate in front of him, piled high with four perfect pancakes, a pat of butter already melting under a generous pour of heated maple syrup. He looked up to thank her, but the sun through the window blazed so bright behind her, he couldn't see her face, which made him sad though he didn't know why. This day was not a day for sadness. Today was an adventure!

The boy quickly ate the pancakes and drank the milk and juice next to the plate. With a deep, satisfying belch he excused himself from the table and dashed out the front door, licking the last of the syrup off his lips as he hummed down the cement walkway that divided their clover-covered lawn exactly in half. He hopped over the short, red picket fence and started down the road, heading for the forest a half-mile away.

The mix of asphalt and pebbled rocks felt good against his bare feet, made him feel like a real man to be able to walk on such terrain without shoes or socks. It hurt a little, but he made sure his face didn't show it, and soon he was walking on the carpet-like cover of the forest floor, Minor's Lettuce and thick giant clover battling over each piece of rich, earthworm-filled dirt. The boy stopped to fiddle through a few clover patches, hoping to find one, but the leaves were three wherever he looked.

A friend of his from first grade once came to school with three separate four-leaf clovers. The boy tested them all himself to make sure they were authentic and not the frauds. Everyone knew you could create a fraud four-leaf by pulling a leaf off two separate threes and then holding the new two-leafs together. These were real. The boy was so excited he made his friend show him exactly where he found them. The boy went there and found nothing special at all and deducted that his friend was a liar and somehow faked the whole thing. The boy hadn't talked to that friend at all in second grade because he didn't like liars or cheats.

The boy slowly made his way deeper into the forest, at first several of the ranch homes still visible here and there through the pines and oaks. He saw a neighbor, a grumpy old white-hair walking the other way, but didn't stop. The man seemed lost in his own thoughts and didn't appear to see the boy. Soon, however, the forest became too thick and the homes too far away to see anything but trees. He stopped then, under a great canopy of giant oak leaves and breathed slow and deep. He imagined the green air flowing into his lungs and coursing down his arms and legs, filling him with natural life. If he hadn't a task, he would have napped then. He still enjoyed a long mid-morning or afternoon nap on a beautiful summer day. But a task such as the one shown in his dream could not be denied for a little boy's nap. He started forward again and remembered.

He was sitting on his favorite rock, a great slate at least as big as his bed that ran at an angle almost too steep for comfort. He had his back to the seasonal stream he called Rainbow Creek and could hear its water splashing against its shallow shores.

Then the water stopped and the boy turned and standing in the middle of the now dry creek bed was a real live leprechaun. A tall, green hat sat atop a dusty, scraggly mop of dark brown hair. The hair grew long, past his narrow shoulders, dusting the green, felt jacket buttoned tightly about him. A rainbow glittered around the three-foot tall, red-bearded, green-eyed man as he winked directly at the boy.

The wink was a magic spell, a spell that told the boy where a pot of gold might be found and a lifetime of luck be reaped.

So the boy woke and ate and came lickety split into the woods to hunt the little creature that had entered his dreams.

Soon, he heard and then saw the stream as it twisted down the slope that would later become a hill and eventually turn into the snow-capped mountain that broke through the trees and shadowed over all the land. The boy didn't have to go that far today, though. His rock was less than a mile up the creek. He'd be there in just a few minutes, ready to test the dream, ready to meet the little man who held the power to change his life, to grant him a real wish.

A ground squirrel scurried across the path - now little more than a deer trail - in front of the boy, startling him and causing him to jump back and almost fall on his rump. There were plenty of rattle snakes in these woods, especially on a warm, sunny day, and it would be just the boy's pre-leprechaun luck to put his foot right on one. He was momentarily confused about how his father let him out of the house without boots but then realized he hadn't asked permission to leave at all. For all they knew, the boy was playing in the front yard with their husky.

"Get," the boy yelled at the squirrel that ignored the boy and continued to chew on the nut or whatever occupied its cheek, forcing him to skirt around the oversized rodent. He was walking backwards, scolding the squirrel when he stepped on the rattlesnake, which immediately sunk both of its long fangs in the soft flesh of the boy's left ankle.

He went down, screaming, in such a state of shock he didn't

remember grabbing the snake by the back of the head, pulling it off his leg and throwing it into the manzanita that grew in abundance along the trail.

A rush of pain and weakness immediately coursed through his leg as his racing heart pumped the snake's poison through the little boy's body. Everything below his thigh felt like a balloon full of needles. He knew he needed to tie something around his leg, but didn't have anything to tie. The bright world dimmed and he fell back, looking up at the deep, blue sky.

I'm going to die, he thought.

"I'll be damned if I let ye die, boy," a voice said, not a high-pitched grating vibration of a voice, but an unexpectedly deep, young-man's voice. Still, even though he could not open his eyes, felt paralyzed completely, the boy knew the leprechaun stood by him.

"One wish me boy, I give ye one wish. And ye know what that one be."

The boy had a different wish in mind, a much better wish, but he couldn't ask it now, couldn't even think it. If he left the world, poisoned by the little snake in the woods, his knew his dad's heart would surely break the rest of the way. He couldn't bring her back this day, and he knew the leprechaun would never return to his place in the woods.

His only wish was to live.

I want to live, he thought. I need to live for my dad. I want to live. I want to live. I wish to live.

When he woke the sun had moved on and nearly set. His mouth felt dry and sour and he rolled over and put his face in the cool water of the little stream. He shook his head and rose from the path, testing his limbs, checking the ankle. It was as if the snake had never been. It was also as if the leprechaun had never been.

He had gotten a wish. A good wish. But not the wish of his heart, the wish that would let him see her face again, smell her skin and touch her hair.

She was still gone.

CHAPTER FOUR – THE LAWN CAN WAIT

I did it again, didn't I? Very sorry about that. I guess I have some issues to work out. Thanks for hanging in there. I promise you'll find something worth squat here any minute.

We never had a great lawn. Before automatic sprinkler systems and lawn care specialists, there was just my brother and me and a broken down, rusty mower and a garden hose ending in a round, steel, hole-poked sprinkler head. The sprinkler was eventually replaced with a lawn bird, which made a nice sound - I remember being lulled to sleep by the click click click, clickety clickety - but the laborers remained the same and the lawn rarely got the attention it needed.

When we moved into the "nice house" in a new development where lawns weren't already planted, grown or installed, we simply didn't have one. So I grew up knowing that the lawn could wait, and did. I've cut down weeds that reached a foot or more over my head. I've deprived my lawn of water during the hottest weeks of summer. I am a habitual lawn abuser and I don't care who knows, because the lawn can wait.

This story has nothing to do with my lawn.

The old man didn't hear his wife when she opened the front door, barely handling the two bags of groceries in her arms as she dipped inside and kicked the door shut, scuttling to the kitchen. She never let the clerks use plastic bags at the store because the straps cut into her hands. He didn't notice her as she put away the soup cans, milk carton, chicken breasts, eggs, rice and the rest. Even

Becoming Dad

though he sat less than five feet from her at the kitchen table, his attention was fully drawn out the small kitchen window.

"George!" she finally yelled, which came out as a harsh screech like a child's cough. He didn't turn but grumbled and batted at the back of his head as if a fly were buzzing about. "You're being rude."

"Lady, you need to shut your trap," he grumbled, still looking out the window. "I saw you when you came in. What do you want me to do, get up and dance?"

"Not rude to me you troll. To our new neighbors."

Now he did turn around and screw up his wrinkled old face at his wife of fifty-five and a half years. "Rude to them?" he threw his thumb behind him. "How am I being rude to them? I can't even see them good through this damn window. You ever going to clean this window, Lady?"

"Well I can see you from outside just fine, and I know they can too. Why don't you give them a chance to move in before you show them what a peep you are?"

George grunted at her and turned back to the window.

"Why'd Jim have to go first? Leave us to go and deal with a new neighbor. Jim was quiet, he took care of the place, and he left me alone! These two are young, Lady, too damn young. They'll have all-hours parties and play all-hours boogie music and leave trash in the driveway. I didn't work at the shop for thirty years to make our two-hundred and thirty-eight dollars and twenty-seven cents payment every single month like a German clock so some hippie could move in next door and turn this neighborhood into a junk yard."

"George you're running red, fool. Stop it before you kill yourself." Her voice still screeched like tires to pavement, but a bit of the aged concern and love showed in the tremor. "I'm sure they are very nice."

George calmed with a couple of deepish breaths and turned back to the window.

"Better be taking good care of Jim's lawn."

The neighbors didn't have wild parties or throw trash on their driveway or play boogie music late at night. They didn't have kids screaming down the street or a hot rod with a deep, rumbling engine. They were quiet and kept to themselves. In fact George rarely saw them as he stared out the kitchen window that his wife still hadn't cleaned.

Four weeks after they moved in, just after Christmas on an icy Saturday morning, George's wife found him very early in the morning, staring out the window, ignoring a chilled cup of coffee and the paper.

"George, for pity's sake," she said. "Those poor people must think you're a lunatic."

"Look at the lawn, Lady. Just look at it."

His wife looked, peering into the scant morning light.

"What of it."

"They haven't mowed it."

"George, it's the middle of winter. How many times have you mowed our grass in the last month?"

"But it needed a trim when they moved in. They haven't touched it."

"I swear to Pete," she said, throwing up her arms and leaving him to his obsession.

In early spring, George's wife came home from a visit with the grandkids across town and found her husband pacing up and down the kitchen in his bedroom robe and slippers, her wax job gone dull in his wake. His head was down and he grumbled with each step.

"George, what's the matter? What's happened?"

He advanced on her pointing his fat, ancient finger.

"I told you, Lady. You said nay, but I told you."

"What, George?"

"The lawn. Have you seen Jim's lawn?"

"I've seen it."

"They haven't cut it once. Not once. It looks like hell."

"George, you stay out of it, hear me?"

He held up three fingers and waved them back and forth. "What's that?"

"Three days, Lady. Three days or I'm going over there to complain. I will not let them ruin this neighborhood, by God."

"You leave those poor people alone, George."

"Three days!" he yelled and stomped down the long hallway to their bedroom for a shower and shave.

The three days came and went and nobody mowed Jim's lawn. George, being held back for several months and three days, waited for his wife to leave the house and then dressed and marched across his perfect lawn, through Jim's neglected jungle and up to the front door of Jim's house. He knocked four perfect, sharp raps.

After several long moments, the door finally opened. A man stuck his head out. He was older than George had guessed, but still very young, probably in his early thirties. His dark hair lay matted against his head and his clothes hung wrinkled and sloppy on his thin body. But he smiled when he saw George and stuck out his hand.

"Hey neighbor," he enthusiastically grabbed George's hand. "I'm Charlie Cochran. Nice to finally meet you."

"Uh, yeah," George said. "Same here. Name's George."

"Nice to meet you George. What can I do you for?"

"Uh, well. Truth is, Charlie, I'm here to complain about Jim's lawn."

"Oh," Charlie looked around at the neighborhood. "Which one is Jim's lawn?"

George wasn't sure if Charlie was making fun.

"Jim's lawn is your lawn," he said. "You're letting it go. You need to mow your lawn."

"My name's Charlie." Charlie let go of George's hand and subconsciously wiped his palm against his thigh.

"I know damn it! Jim is dead. This was his house. You aren't taking care of his lawn." George's face was turning red again.

"Oh, I see," Charlie lowered his head. "Well, I should go,

George."

"What about the Lawn?"

Charlie looked up and smiled again.

"The lawn can wait," he said and slammed the door.

George watched the neighbor's lawn grow through the wet months and right into summer. He paced his house and yelled at the window. He complained daily to his wife who shushed him and told him to mind his own business. He even called the police one day, but they told him bad lawn care was not a crime.

As the hot months came on and the rains dried up for the year Jim's lawn quickly died. By mid-summer it was nothing but long, dead grass and hard, cracked earth, and George felt as if he would go crazy if he didn't confront the lazy bum next door.

One day in mid August, George walked across his perfect lawn and through what used to be a lawn and up to the front door at Jim's house. Again he knocked hard and sharp and again after too long the door finally opened.

"Hello George," Charlie said with a half smile. "What is it?" Charlie was dressed much as before and the house was dark inside.

George turned and presented the yard.

"This," he said. "First you won't cut the lawn. Now you just let it die? What the hell? This used to be a nice neighborhood. Now, thanks to you, mister, it looks like hell."

"I gotta go, George." Charlie sighed heavily. "Is there anything else?"

"Yeah, give it some water. Turn on your sprinklers for God sake."

"The lawn can wait," Charlie said and again, slammed the door.

Four days later George woke early in the morning to a flashing red light. He rose from his bed, put on his robe, relieved himself and walked to the kitchen, where the light was strongest. He looked outside and saw an ambulance and fire truck outside Jim's house. It was so much like the scene after Jim died, George thought for a moment he might be dreaming. But when he saw his neighbor walking out of his house, one hand on a white blanket covering someone lying on a gurney as two EMTs wheeled it towards the ambulance, he knew it was real.

Every instinct in George's old and feeble mind told him to stay in his house, and when he reached for the front door he felt as if he was pushing against air as thick as water. As he walked across his perfect lawn and then across the barren wasteland of Jim's old lawn his mind turned over, dizziness threatening to knock him down.

He reached his neighbor just as they were putting the body in the ambulance.

"Charlie," he said, his voice cracked. Charlie turned and looked at him, a face covered with tears, eyes distant and lost.

"Charlie," the old man said again. "Was that your wife?"

"Missy's had cancer now for seven years," Charlie finally said. "She's fought it so hard. Almost had it once. Total remission. But there was a tumor they missed. Started as breast cancer you know. Did the whole mastectomy thing. Then, a year ago, out of the blue, she says she wants to move back here, to this town where she grew up and buy a house in the neighborhood where she used to play. Well, what's a guy to do?" He shrugged, a fresh pour of tears spilling down his cheeks. "I quit my job, bought this place, moved four hundred miles and gave her a few months here, looking out her window." He looked hard at the old man. "Like you George."

Charlie turned his back on George and started walking back towards Jim's house.

"I'll get on the lawn tomorrow, George."

CHAPTER FIVE – DAD'S IN THE KITCHEN

Like George, my father learned the lesson very late not to make assumptions about what's going on in someone else's life. I'm still working on it, but I think I'm getting better.

Some years back, sister number four put together a cookbook called "Howie's in the Kitchen." She had spent an afternoon on our dad's deathbed taking notes on the recipes we enjoyed so much, and years later gave it to all of us for Christmas. We like to make each other cry at Christmas. I cherish that book and all the memories of my father being the chef of our family. And I am so proud to be that man for my children.

That was a bit much, wasn't it? But it's true. Let's move this wagon, shall we?

Allie stood in front of the well-dressed crowd seated at the round tables littered with the remnants of a gourmet meal. The last of them eased off their applause and a bright silence swept through the dimly lit auditorium.

She stood at a short, dark granite podium and felt the expectation of the well-dressed board members sitting on the stage behind her. Her speech swam through her head, opening thesis, bullet points, memorable phrases. But one thought kept pushing all the preparation and rehearsal away, scrambling it all until she could concentrate on nothing else.

Tell the truth.

How could she? After twenty years of building the

association to this, why would she jeopardize her reputation and the momentum of her work by telling a story no one would believe anyway? What purpose would it serve? None. None at all.

Tell the truth.

The whispers had begun six months earlier when Carlita, there almost from the beginning, told her how they were going to raise half a million dollars for the African relief.

"Sweetie," she had said in her way that made Allie feel more than four years younger. She stood, arms crossed in their modest apartment on the 9th floor of a building in New York City. She stood nearly half a foot taller, her dark perfect face framing perfect black eyes that looked into the deepest part of Allie. Allie loved her passionately, even after twenty years, and already knew she would do whatever Carlita asked.

"It's simple mathematics. You get five hundred people together for some chow and charge each of them a thou a plate. That's half a mill and enough to support our Africa outfit for the next five years. Think about it. We'll invite all the movie industry folks, all the political camp, the Richy Rich's. We'll sell out, I guarantee it."

"They'll never come Car. Why would they?"

"Honey please," she wrapped her dark arms around Allie's much smaller, yellow-skinned frame. "Your story is *the* story. Hell, we could sell a thousand plates. More!"

Tell the truth.

Allie had agreed easily enough to be the center of attention for the evening, but to her own shame it wasn't because of the children it would feed. Like a criminal who never got caught but instead carried their crime with them through life, whispering at their happiness, Allie had a secret and could no longer keep it to herself.

She prepared a false story of course, an interesting, soulful, tale of a girl who learned to appreciate three squares through the teachings of an aged grandmother who had starved nearly to death in the great depression. This was her just-in-case story, her fall back in case she lost her nerve and decided not to put her sanity up for debate by the entire world.

Allie did not lie, which was the reason for her silence all this time. If she simply stayed silent about her past she wouldn't have to reveal anything that might put question to her calling. But instead of directing attention away from her past, it made her seem mysterious. And as her visibility grew, as the progress of the association swept across the continents, as the palpable reality of her programs to feed starving communities across the world materialized almost of its own volition, the story of her life and inspiration became the subject of speculation, investigation and then obsession.

And Allie knew why Carlita had thought of the scheme in the first place. Because Carlita didn't know either. If she had to find out the truth about her true love at the same time as five hundred celebrities, dignitaries and rich folk, then so be it.

And that last thought was why she decided to tell the real story, for better or worse. She owed it to Carlita. She looked across the sea of important people and focused on her love, at the front table beside the empty seat she had just vacated. Carlita smiled her big, bright, white-toothed smile and blew Allie a kiss.

"Thank you all," Allie said. "Your donation tonight will help fund programs that will feed communities all across Africa for generations to come. My cause is now your cause and I thank you with all my heart." That was Allie's thing she said. My cause is now your cause. That simple phrase put an obligation on those who heard it. Like a curse in reverse, once Allie said that to someone, they were bound to help, unable to argue against it. Unwilling to resist.

"I came here tonight with a prepared story of how I got to be here. I've never been comfortable with the attention my past has been given and I'm ready to put it to rest. But the story I prepared is not the truth." Some of the smiles turned to frowns, like little lights going out on an auditorium sized Christmas tree. "I need to tell the truth, no matter what you think of me afterwards." Carlita's smile had not faded, although Allie could see a slight strain in her eyes, a fear of what was to come.

Allie grew up in a suburban home in Hollywood as Tiali Lee, an only daughter of a rich plastic surgeon father and a mother who spent more time on vacation, away from Tiali, than home. A young, black woman took care of Tiali more often than not. Her name was Margaret and Tiali thought she might have died of sadness if it weren't for her care.

Margaret was not just a nanny. She was also a cook. She would create feasts three times a day for the two of them to share, meals with several courses and a variety of wondrous flavors. She would bake warm, dark breads and flaky biscuits. And she would prepare homemade desserts that would make Tiali squeal with pleasure as she sat up, propped on ten pillows on a bed of down, holding a bowl of something sweet in three ways, licking a spoon dripping with child ecstasy.

Tiali had everything she could want, was spoiled rotten by her life. And may have continued that way for all of her mortal existence. But one day after school, she came into their giant home and found Margaret with another woman who could only be her mother. The other woman had a dark, thick smell coming off her, dressed in layers and shreds of multi-colored fabrics, faded and dirty, but holding together. Her black hair had grown matted and wild, as wild as her eyes. She was screaming at her child and Tiali soon realized she was the subject of the rant.

"Child, you have done her wrong. What you tinking? You gone soft here child? Don't make mama ashamed of what she brought to this world. You do her right. She has more important tings to do than eat herself trough life, much more important, child."

Margaret stood in her white uniform with her hands folded before her, her head down.

"I will mama," she said.

That night, unbeknownst to Tiali's absent parents,

Margaret's mom took the guesthouse. Tiali woke in the deepest part of the darkest hour to the sound of two women chanting outside her window. She walked down the stairs in her pajamas, opened the back door and approached the fire burning in the back of the house, a small, intense purplish flame burning from something other than wood. It burned from a bronze brazier between the ladies who danced like animals and chanted words Tiali had never heard. They both now wore the colorful rags, their feet bare, their hair wild.

They took the young girl's hands and pulled her around the fire so fast that she thought she might stumble. But she managed to stay upright and run around the purple flame. Their chanting grew in speed and volume and Tiali feared her parents' neighbors might wake and discover them.

Then the two women began chanting something new, something she did understand.

"My cause is now your cause. My cause is now your cause," they said over and over, spinning her faster and faster around the flame. And just when Tiali thought she might vomit from the motion, they stopped and did the most unthinkable thing she could imagine. They swung her back away from the purple flame and then forward, directly at it, releasing her at the top of the arc so she was flying right at it with no hope to avoid injury.

"And that's when I began the journey," Allie said to the quiet crowd. "I don't know how many days I was gone, or how many places I visited. I don't know how it was accomplished or what happened to the two women who sent me. But my life was forever changed.

"You see, I was transformed, if that's the right word, across the planet, and into the lives, into the existences of children everywhere. Somehow those two gave me the gift of seeing through the eyes of others, feeling their pains, the tightness of their bellies, the ravages of their diseases, the anguish in their hearts. I could smell the stench of the death around me, the spoiling of life, the misery with every breath they took. I felt them each die.

"I can't tell you how many times I died that night, if it was a night. Sometimes it felt as if I were in one child's existence for weeks as they slowly faded to nothing. Sometimes they would suffocate quickly and painfully from some illness that ravaged their lungs or their heart beyond recovery. But they were all children, about my age.

Allie took in a slow, sighing breath as she studied the black podium, unable to look at the people who had come to hear her story.

"When I woke, Margaret and her mom were gone as was the brazier, although I could see the circle of dead grass where it had been. Within a year, I had stolen enough money from my parents to set out on my own, to begin my second life. I was twelve years old when I left." Allie laughed, a tear falling down her cheek. "When I imagine the little, meek, twelve-year-old Asian girl with ten thousand dollars in cash setting out to change the world, it is beyond absurd. But that is exactly what happened. I do not lie."

She steeled herself and looked up at the crowd, ready for the ridicule in their eyes. For a moment no one moved. Carlita was not in her seat. Allie's worst fear of losing her love had come true. Panic knotted in her throat.

Then she caught a dark figure on the stage to her right and turned to focus on Carlita, standing there, beautiful as light, smiling. Carlita wrapped her up in her arms and hugged her with stifling strength.

"You could have told me," she whispered quietly in her ear as the audience erupted in enthusiastic applause.

"I was afraid," Allie said.

"They don't believe it, you know. They think you made it up and they love it. They are used to being wowed. Your real story has done more for the association tonight than anything you could have made up. We are going to help so many more people."

Allie hugged her back as hard as she could.

"I love you, Car."

"I love you too, little one. My cause is your cause."

CHAPTER SIX – SIXTY DOLLARS

I wasn't a particularly honest boy. I don't know if the learned restraint about the deeper feelings of my mom had anything to do with it, but after chapters one and three, I have my suspicions.

I liked to snoop around in my dad's closet, search the shelves and rummage through any containers left unlocked and unattended. I enjoyed digging into his bathroom drawers and opening forgotten, dirt-covered boxes in the carport just to find what I might find.

I lied a lot. I'd spin tales for my friends of feats I didn't do, girls I hadn't kissed, fights I never fought. I'd lie to my siblings and teachers, even perfect strangers. I'd lie when the lie wasn't necessary, served no purpose, as if I were honing a skill, practicing for when it really counted. It's ironic because dishonesty now is very difficult for me. It's as if people only have so many untruths within them and I used mine up before I could vote.

I stole candy cigarettes and Vienna sausages from the local market, broke into little mom and pop businesses on the weekend to play with their merchandise and liked to take match to a wide variety of flora and plastic toy to see how they would burn.

For several years of childhood my father worked out of town. He would leave Monday morning and get back Friday night. He was an actual traveling salesman (see Chapter 21.) Sister number two - internal editor - has also been my mother since shortly after my fifth birthday. She moved in with us at the age of twenty-three, herself already a single mom, because the three youngest sibs still required some serious baking.

At about the age of nine or ten during one of my snoops, I learned that the pants my father took off Friday night, hanging over a chair in his bedroom, contained cash. He, like most men, enjoyed having a wad in his front right pocket, including ones, fives, tens and twenties with the occasional coveted hundred-dollar bill.

I also learned taking a few dollars from that wad went unnoticed.

Every week I took money from my dad's pants. I could see him in his recliner, watching golf, the path to his bedroom a dash across his peripheral vision. I'd peak around the corner of the hallway, playing James Bond, waiting for him to light his pipe or get on the phone. The second he was distracted, I'd dash across, quickly flip through his roll of green, grab what I thought wouldn't be detected and run back to my room.

I just realized what all these dishonesties have in common.

The thrill.

The thrill is what drove me to eventually overstep and commit a crime that could not be ignored.

Sounds ominous, doesn't it?

It's not.

In the small-town neighborhood where the boy grew up, one of his favorite places to visit was Sam's Bike Shop. He liked it because it was less a store and more a shed behind an old man's house. He liked it because the bikes weren't new. Like his own first bike, purchased from Sam's backyard by his father, these two-wheelers were used and forgotten when the old man purchased them for nothing. He painted, rebuilt, lubed up and displayed them on heavy hooks in a line under the tin awning of his store.

Boys would come to Sam's shop and gawk the afternoon away, smell the fresh grease on old gears, spin the front wheels hanging in mid-air and run the cranks of the bikes clutched by Sam's homemade, giant vise. The boys gawked, but few ever purchased anything. Our boy was one of the lucky few whose parent knew about Sam and had thrown down some green for the purchase of Big Blue, a massive, steel, one-geared beast with a giant, springy, triangle seat and flat steel bars, riding on fat, slick, white-walled tires.

The boy loved his bike, knew he was the fastest kid on the

block with Blue under him, rode it daily no matter the weather. But he loved the red one more.

The Red One. The beautiful, cherry-red ten-speed with a black, narrow seat and handlebars full of gears and brakes. The boy knew Sam had rebuilt the bike, but couldn't detect any difference from the new one in the Sears Wish Book. Its wheels turned true, its handlebars were square and its chrome gleamed as if it were shined that morning.

But the Red One also had the biggest price tag in Sam's yard, $59.99, a small fortune for a fifth grader without a job.

"My Dad's going to buy that one," he told Sam one day after the other boys had gone home. A mountain chill had settled in the air as autumn twilight crept across the sky. "He told me yesterday he was going to buy it."

Sam, a small frail man with glasses that took up half his face and no more than a sprig of hair wisping around the top of his pointed little head, smiled widely, showing off a perfect set of false teeth.

"I'm sure he did," he said. "Any idea when he's going to take this beauty off my hands?"

"Yeah, sure. He said next week." The boy shuffled his feet and blushed a bit with the fib, but Sam didn't say anything. "He's gonna give me the money."

"Well, I'll be looking forward to it. Now get going, boy. I'm done today."

That all happened on a Saturday night. The boy's father was leaving Monday morning for his week working in the city. He knew he didn't have much time.

That night after dinner, the boy sitting on the living room couch, enjoying a root beer frozen pop with his father and settling in for the Walt Disney Movie of the Week, he made his first sweep.

"Hey Dad," he said. "Robbie's getting a ten speed for his birthday."

"Mmhmm," his dad mumbled. Strike one.

"He said his mom is buying him a ten speed. Yeah. And it's

going to cost a hundred dollars!"

"Really?" Strike two. His father was not listening at all. The boy knew he either had to shake things up or give it up. He got off the couch, stood in front of the little color television and crossed his arms.

"Son?"

"Dad, do you want to save forty dollars or what?"

"Well, sure I do. What's the scoop?"

"Dad! Weren't you listening?"

"You bet I was. You think you're going to talk me into buying you a ten speed just after I bought you the bike you have, a fine bike, a solid bike, because either your buddy is getting one or I can somehow come out forty bucks ahead, or possibly both? That about cover it?"

"Nevermind!" the boy yelled and stomped off to his room.

The boy had taken one or two dollars from his father's pants maybe two dozen times over the past year. The most he ever lifted was a five-dollar bill, but that was only because he found several fives and thought it wouldn't be missed.

But sixty dollars.

There was simply no thinking about it. Shortly after 11:35PM when Johnny was still on his monologue, the boy dashed into his father's room. His heart slamming against his little rib cage, the light from the hallway bathroom showing his way, he found his dad's slacks, as always, draped across the big chair in his room. He slipped his hand in the front pocket and found nothing but keys. After a moment of sheer panic he realized he had the wrong pocket and tried the other. His fingers slipped around a thick wad of bills. The television had gone to a commercial and the boy feared his dad would catch him mid-theft.

There were several ones and fives and six twenty-dollar bills. He took three and put the rest back, ducked down low and darted back to his room.

That night, it took the boy three full hours to fall asleep.

The next morning he stayed in bed until he heard the

Cadillac's engine turn and thunder into existence. Within a couple of minutes, he was ready for school and running for the bus stop.

The boy might have gotten away with his heist, at least for the day, if he hadn't shown the three twenties to every single kid in school, bragging about the bike he was about to buy. Word got to the teachers and the teachers called the hotel where his dad was staying. He didn't get the bike. In fact, the teachers confiscated the sixty bucks before the day was out.

But the boy learned two things from that experience and never stole another dollar from his father.

First, he learned his father wasn't as stupid as he thought. And second, he realized his father had his back. That night he called home just after dinner, asking to speak to his son. The boy took the receiver, hand shaking.

"So, I got a call from your teacher, today."

"Yeah."

"Apparently, I made a mistake when I gave you your lunch money for the week."

"Uh, yeah."

"I'm pretty embarrassed by this. Let's just keep it between you and me. I'll pick up the money from your school on Friday. Deal?"

And he never mentioned it again.

CHAPTER SEVEN - LOCKJAW

Okay, I'm not implying it was a good thing my dad avoided punishing me at all costs and gave me excuses for my crimes I could never myself dream up. What the hell am I saying? Of course I am. That was one of the best parts of growing up in my house, the pure lack of supervision. I loved it and wouldn't change it for the world, and you're all jealous you couldn't get away with half the things I got away with as a boy. And because of what I did, my poor children have a dad who watches them constantly and suspects foul play in everything they do.

Seriously, though, it was pretty cool.

To me the word lockjaw is synonymous with belief or faith in what one is told as truth.

One day in my seventh year I was playing with some friends at the ballpark in my hometown. We weren't playing ball, we were looking for an adventure. The adults were playing ball. We were searching for towers to climb and fences to scale and dirt clods to throw at passing cars. I managed to find a long strand of rusty barbed wire with my leg.

The adults, after a dutiful examination of my long, jagged wound (probably not that long and fairly straight) proclaimed I needed a tetanus shot within twenty-four hours or I could get lockjaw. "What is lockjaw," I asked. "It's when you can't move your jaw and you die," they warned. "Oh shit," I said. We all know I didn't say that, but wouldn't it have been great if I did?

So I started counting the hours. It was fairly early in the day and if I had twenty-four hours, I was going to have to get that shot first thing the next day or I might die. I fell asleep that night moving my jaw back and forth, praying I'd survive till morning. I woke sister number two at first light as if Santa had come to town, insisting she take me to get my shot.

"You're not going to fall over and die from lockjaw," she said and went back to sleep.

Now, in my little mind I really did think I was going to fall over and die. I thought I was dust, doomed. I thought at the very least I'd have to eat through a straw for the rest of my life. I spent the morning by myself, moving my jaw, loading up on Wonder bread and peanut butter so I could live longer if my mouth stopped working. I didn't get a shot, I didn't get lockjaw and all I got from all the white bread and Skippy was an upset stomach.

Which brings us to the seventh story.

There once was a boy who believed everything any adult ever told him. If an adult said it, he believed it. They were older after all, and bigger, smarter and they wore fancier clothes. Why would they say it if it weren't true?

He believed that an oversized rabbit named Pete managed to cover every hillside, every yard and every living room with colored eggs once a year. This oversized freak-of-nature also, somehow, carried along with him a basket for every child filled to the rim with jelly beans and chocolate bunnies, chewy fruity things and chocolate covered bits of sugar, all floating on top of a bed of plastic grass that his mom somehow found in the carpet six months after Pete's visit. He believed it because the adults said it was true.

He believed that a spooky old man in a red suit with a giant black belt and a massive white beard spent an entire year in freezing conditions with an army of little people, making all the toys every single child got for Christmas. And this guy had real talent because he was able to make the toys in the same packages as the boy saw at the store, with the same names, and the same small arsenal of batteries to make sure these wonders would move and talk and roll and pee when they were supposed to. He knew that the scary fat man got to each home by soaring along in a sleigh pulled by flying deer. He tried real hard to be good every year because the scary man also brought along a bag of coal and rotten carrots that he sometimes had to give to the bad kids. The boy knew a few of those kids too and was always afraid to ask what they got from Santa, because he knew it must be black and dirty. He believed it because his parents and aunts and uncles and grandparents all said it was true.

They wouldn't say it otherwise.

This boy believed in the magic of dragons and wizards because when he asked his father if they were real, his father said, "Of course they are." He never saw one though because they didn't live in neighborhoods with houses and sidewalks. They lived in castles and someday the boy was going to go see them. He also believed in UFO's and aliens because once his dad had told him that he actually saw one flying in the sky, "faster than anything I've ever seen." And why would he say it if it wasn't true?

The boy knew ghosts to be real because his sister once had a séance and a ghost made a door slam and a hanging pot sway. The ghost spoke through his sister and said he had been murdered and he couldn't rest until he completed his unfinished business. The boy felt bad for the ghost, but was afraid of him. He knew ghosts were real because his sister was much older than he was and she wouldn't say it if it wasn't true.

The boy believed in vampires, goblins and ogres. He had seen movies with these creatures and nobody said it was make-believe. Once a year many of these creatures roamed about, along with witches and warlocks. He was afraid and stayed close to his sister when they went begging for candy in the neighborhood.

He believed that Christopher Columbus was the guy who discovered America and that George Washington chopped down a tree and got completely busted by his dad. He believed in a giant man named Paul who had a giant blue bovine following him around and one day they got in a wrestling match and made the Grand Canyon. He knew that Davey Crockett was the king of the wild frontier and Tarzan was the king of the apes and thought Davey would win that battle because he'd just shoot Tarzan dead before he could call his animal buddies. He believed that now that slavery was abolished, thank goodness solely to Abraham Lincoln, black people and white people got along as well as anyone else. Adults told him all these things and he believed it.

From the stories of his elders, the boy quickly learned that if you don't look both ways before you cross the street, you are going to die. If you don't brush and floss your teeth every day, you'll look like grandpa with his fake teeth before you finish high school. If you eat and go swimming you will get a cramp and drown. And if you touch yourself and enjoy it you will slowly, completely go blind.

In the wilderness, moss only grew on the north side of trees and bears wouldn't bother you if you just played like you were dead already. Black widow spiders and scorpions would kill you in a second if given the chance. A ground hog's shadow meant more days of cold and a rattlesnake liked to bite little boys in particular. If he ever got lost in the woods, he'd be ready because the adults told him what was what.

He learned that politicians were the most noble of men, leading our great country into more greatness. They knew better than others, were heroes, kind and powerful, giants of giants. Their word was law. Policemen were always, always there to protect a boy like him, or anyone else because they kept the peace. Professional athletes were an inspiration to all; their bodies were machines of perfection, their love for their fans never ended.

And the boy believed in God. He believed in a robed, bearded man floating somewhere up there, looking down on every human being, taking care of them, listening to their prayers and helping them with their lives. The preachers all told him that God had a son who died a gruesome death nailed to a cross so that the boy's sins would be eradicated. When the boy sat in a church surrounded by stained glass and pious people, he knew that God hovered right over his head, watching him and smiling. He prayed to God a lot, mostly when he wanted something he knew he could not have. And it was nice having God there to listen. Because otherwise he would be talking to himself and feel foolish. It was easier to talk to God. And most everyone he knew told him God was real, so he believed it completely.

And the boy grew and became a man. He was a good man who worked hard and provided. He led those he could lead and loved those he would love. He should have been a very happy man.

Except for Peter Cottontail and Santa Claus. Save for Dragons and Wizards, UFO's, ghosts and a host of creepy creatures. Considering Columbus, Washington, Paul and Blue, Davey Crocket, Tarzan and Abraham Lincoln. The rules of life or death, the credo of the great outdoors, the godlike men and God himself.

Slowly and surely, as he became a man, the boyhood knowledge was left behind. He didn't feel joy as the childish, childhood beliefs were stripped away. Sad and forlorn at first, the man finally became resolved and did what most every adult does, generation after generation.

He had children and told them all the stories, used his father-authority to make them believe in everything he believed as a child. And for better or worse, the cycle continued.

CHAPTER EIGHT – SPAGHETTI SAUCE

Not sure what to think about that last one. I'm not nearly as cynical as that may have made me sound. I wouldn't be writing this if I were a pessimist. I like to have fun just as much as the next guy.

Speaking of fun, let's talk about obscene hand gestures.

I remember the first time I flipped the bird. Does everyone remember that moment, or is it just me?

I was eight years old and had just recently discovered the difference between thumbs up and middle finger up; one the Fonz did and the other he did not. I practiced in my room or sitting on the toilet, marveling at how vulgar my own finger could look when it stood all by itself. I loved it and felt tough. I realized that with my one finger I could shock my teachers, defy my father and intimidate the bullies. Wouldn't it be great for a skinny little eight-year-old boy if that were actually true?

A few weeks went by before I got the opportunity to use my newfound form of communication. But inevitably, the moment arrived.

The days had grown longer than the nights and the icy white was replaced by a hundred hues of green. Spring fever is a real thing to a child in a cold, snowy climate. It hits hard as concrete shrapnel and there is absolutely nothing a boy can do to keep his head.

So, I was in the middle of the euphoria of the season and I remembered my finger. I sat at my desk in class and ignored Mrs. Shiplet, obsessing and fantasizing about when I would have the opportunity to begin world domination.

The chance was less than an hour away.

During recess, when the Spring fever set in, the boys of third and fourth grade at East Burney Elementary would gather on the faded, gravelly asphalt around the yellow, painted diamond and play kick ball. It was my first experience with competitive sports and I performed much as I do in all competitive sports. Mainly, like a girl. The only reason I get away with that comment is I have a sister who can beat me at literally every sport. No, that one also. Seriously.

So anyway, I'm terrified as always and up to kick. And who is pitching but my former friend, Pat the fourth grader.

Pat and I had logged a good number of hours as friends. We lived only a couple of blocks from each other and during the entire previous summer could barely be found apart. But then something went awry, something awful, something dreadful, something so terrible that on that spring day looking at my new nemesis/old friend getting ready to hurl a ball at, probably, my head, I couldn't remember what that something was.

And worse, Pat had hooked up with Jerry. Jerry was bigger than most fourth graders, and older, which I guess go together. I had no doubt that he could probably lift me up with one hand, by my skull, and bash it against the school's brick exterior.

Jerry was playing first base.

Did I mention I could not kick the ball?

And these guys hated me?

And I was wearing corduroy pants and Hush Puppy Shoes and an orange, yellow and brown horizontally striped shirt?

So Pat wound up and took a shot at my brain, barely missing. But he knows he gets three or four swings and his evil smile has not faltered one iota. Ball one. Okay, here comes another one. This one hits me square in the chest. I supposed I could have dodged - hey I was playing dodge ball and I didn't even know it - the red bounce of pain, but I was too scared to move. Ball two. Pat's laughing, but I can tell if he doesn't really hurt me with this next shot he's going to get pissed and sic Jerry on me next recess. Pat winds up, leans back and lets the thing go with everything he has.

Bad throw.

I could tell it was a bad throw because it went right to my foot. I didn't so much kick it as it ricochet off my foot. The red menace came back at Pat's head and he had to duck to the ground to avoid it. And to make matters worse, it skipped into the outfield, far from Pat or Jerry or any of their teammates.

I ran to first base. Jerry tried to trip me and failed. Did I mention Jerry was not the brightest bulb on the Christmas tree?

I ran to second and third as well before the ball made it back into the infield.

Standing on third, exhilarated, panting, bent over and gripping my knees, I looked at Pat, and smiled.

The look Pat returned was a mix of rage and anticipation. Jerry's attention was already lost to a spring bug zipping by his head, but Pat had enough devil in his stare for both of them. I realized I was going to get seriously pounded, possibly even hurt. What to do, what to do...

Almost of its own volition the middle finger of my right hand shot skyward.

The act didn't have the life-altering, mind-controlling effect I had hoped for. And thinking back over the years of my life, I have never had much success with this particular expression. It may be a lofty, go-to-hell in New York, but in California's north state, it apparently meant, "Please kick my ass." With that single motion, I have had a knife, ax and gun pulled on me, not all at once of course. I have been driven off the road and chased on foot several times. I can't think of one single time when the result of flipping the bird was a positive experience. And this was the first of many.

And it all came down to spaghetti sauce. Doesn't it always come down to spaghetti sauce, sooner or later?

That night, I learned something about myself, about how I would manage confrontations for the rest of my life. My sister - who was watching the three youngest sibs as she often did - wanted to make spaghetti. I know now the reason for this is because it's cheap and easy to make and can feed a hungry hoard of kids. At the time, all I knew was she needed a jar of Ragu to complete her feast and for some reason I had been chosen to ride my bike down to the corner market and retrieve the red.

Having survived the rest of the day at school and running home - I could run much faster than either of them at their best - from the bus stop, I felt the day had played out, that tomorrow things would be different and hell, Pat and I may even become friends again.

I was tooling towards Lyle's market on my single speed steel beast, the sun just disappearing over the high mountain in the western sky, two dollars crumpled in my right hand, when I heard, "Get him!"

Exactly! I know! We should have ordered pizza!

I see the dark figures behind me, who had actually been lying in wait near my house for me to come out.

I'm sure I mentioned in chapter six that I was the absolute fastest thing on two wheels in my neighborhood. One speed or ten, I could beat anyone, especially these two. I stood up and pumped my legs as hard as I could, flying down the road, feeling like I was challenging the cars driving past me, my pursuers soon left far behind.

Once inside the store I realized my mistake.

Now there were two of them, outside, probably waiting by my bike, ready to take me out. I purchased the Ragu jar and a piece of gum with the few pennies left over, faced the exit, took a deep breath and plunged into the near-dark.

They were nowhere.

I jumped on my bike and raced back towards my house. Pat appeared behind me. I actually yelled, "You can't catch me," as I stretched the distance between our two bikes. Yes, I did feel a little like the gingerbread man.

Until I saw Jerry, who was waiting beside the road, directly in my path, standing with his bike crosswise in front of him, blocking my advance. As I got within fifty feet I slowed down.

Forty...thirty. I was now barely moving forward, showing him that he had me beat. Twenty...ten...five. At five feet, almost at a standstill, I pumped once on my pedals, hard, and drove my bike directly into the road. Luck was with me and there was no traffic at the time, which would have been my undoing because it was a four-lane highway.

Jerry rolled his bike after me, which missed. After traveling a good distance it fell in the middle of the highway and rattled across the heavy asphalt.

I sped home, presented the jar to my sister with more pride than she could understand and thoroughly enjoyed my cheap, spaghetti dinner.

I learned three things that day. First, it's better to outsmart the big, violent, dumb guy than to try and take him on. Second, spaghetti is a pretty good victory dinner and only costs a couple bucks. And third, flipping the bird is a bad idea, no matter what the circumstance. Well, I didn't actually learn that lesson until much later, like last week.

CHAPTER NINE – BE BRAVE

My dad was one of the bravest men to ever walk the planet. We all think that of our fathers, don't we? The only thing he ever feared was confronting his kids, poor guy. But bravery, real bravery is manifested not with sword and shield and spiked helm. Real bravery is a woman raising her first child after her second is stillborn. It's a man who maintains his composure and dignity after being told his cancer is mortal and he'll be gone in ninety days. It's a black man who is true to himself in a white world, or a white man who is secure in a black world. It's a lesbian couple walking hand in hand and pushing a stroller carrying their adopted son down an immaculate sidewalk in an immaculate neighborhood on the outskirts of an immaculately conservative town. It's a child who comforts his mother when she's sad and alone because all she ever does is work and raise her son. These people are brave. They are the strongest of humankind.

Children make a father brave and cowardly all at the same time. There is nothing I wouldn't do for my children, no sacrifice I wouldn't make, nothing I wouldn't give them of myself. But I am terrified - the kind of scaredy-cat terrified that nearly paralyzes me - about what harm might come to my kids. I thought the feeling would lessen as they grew out of the first few years, but they are always in harm's way, in a much bigger and more serious harm's way as they push against adulthood.

The woman shuffled down the sidewalk, which ran along a cold dead street devoid of light and warmth. No traffic busied the black asphalt and no other souls walked the night. Bent with age and other things, the woman pulled her rags tight about her,

fending off the chill with greasy fabric of a hundred dull colors which hung loosely all about her. Her black hair stood in haphazard clumps running this way and that across her head, which bowed hatless against the icy air.

A puff of steamy breath preceded her; a coughing fit racking her chest with dry hacks and wheezes, the latest symptoms of her reaper, the pneumonia that had been chasing her for almost two months.

Normally, if she had a normal anymore, she would hide away in the mission for the night. They usually let her in during cold snaps even though she wouldn't abide by their religious talk and wouldn't walk into their chapel. They would say to her, because it was their calling, that she could have a bowl of watery soup and a piece of stale bread with a hot cup of weak coffee to wash it all down, if she would just sit through a thirty minute sermon in the chapel. She would say no thank you very much, may I please spend the night. And they would let her, even though they weren't supposed to. She knew why. They thought she had some power over them and their lives. They thought she was a black witch from New Orleans because of her accent and her eyes. She was no witch, of course, but she had a sense and felt she could influence people when she needed to. If only she could have influenced herself when it mattered.

Another coughing fit took her almost to her knees and the woman noticed a splash of bright red on her dirty sleeve. It hadn't been the first time she'd seen blood in her cough. But this was clear, almost as if her heart had just pumped it out.

"Numo," she said when she could. "Numo, you leave me 'lone tonight. Its hour's mine you swine. I be yours when de sun shines bright."

Numo laughed, his voice deep and powerful, if not evil.

"Gretta, you will be with me when I determine it."

Gretta walked in silence for a moment.

"Hell, just give me an' mine an hour den, why doncha?"

Numo's next words were conversational, as if they were

friends sharing lunch.

"I don't know what you think this will get you anyway, Gretta. You might as well be walking off a cliff for all it matters. You think something good will come of this? I'm here to tell you it won't. Not for you, not for him. Believe me. I've seen it more times than I can count. It's a bad way to spend this hour you're begging for."

"I ain't beggin'."

"Okay then, asking. Let's go down and walk through the park, look at the stars and the moon. Let's go do something fun, like freak out the late nighters on the subway. Might as well get the most of this. You could put on a real show."

"You givin' me de hour?"

"Yeah, yeah, okay. The hour is yours. Why not? I guess one could say you deserve it."

"Tanks Numo. You ah a real gentleman."

"You know it," he said and left her alone.

As she walked, Gretta's life walked across her mind.

She was born not twenty miles from the road she now walked, in a four story brick building the residents called Trinity Hall, although she never learned why. She lived her first five years in that building with her mother, a waitress who smoked more than a pack of ciggys a day and coughed like she might expel a lung any moment. She remembered brief glimpses of her father, mostly his giant brown hands and the snowy teeth of his smile. But by the time she was five he was no longer a part of her life.

They got kicked out of Trinity Hall while she was in kindergarten and that was the last she ever saw of school. Her mom said they booted them because they were black, but Gretta knew better, even at that age. She knew her mom smoked more than cigarettes and that drugs were not allowed.

So they traveled around a bit. Gretta felt hungry a lot, but never said anything to her mom, who was often too far gone to hear her daughter anyway. They settled in a house that used to be a mansion but was now just a place where people would go to smoke their stuff and hide from the cops. Gretta was eight when they moved there, taking one of the back rooms, away from most of the action. One lady, sort of a clean-up person who would make sure the rooms were clear and the people who needed to be out were out, started looking after Gretta, giving her bits of food when she had it and making sure she was in bed at night. She even gave Gretta a pair of shoes once that almost fit. Gretta didn't dare ask where they came from.

Gretta had just turned nine when her mom died. She felt sad about her dying, but not very sad. By the time she overdosed she was barely a person anymore. She just sat, her eyes flat, against a dirty wall and smoked her pipe or stabbed needles into her arms. Gretta had come to rely on the lady, who she only called Lady, for her basic needs anyway. The only thing her mom ever gave her was an ugly accent.

At eleven years old, Gretta started smoking cigarettes. At fourteen, Lady gave her a hit off a crack pipe and by fifteen she was shooting heroin and crack almost every day. She soon discovered that she could have as much as she wanted if she let men do their thing with her. So she let them because it was easy and because she needed her stuff.

It was all going pretty fine by her mind until some asshole decided he didn't want to wear a rubber and got her pregnant.

Gretta, who had never done any one thing for any one person in her short little life, checked into a free clinic and went through detox, which she thought would kill her or the baby or both. But it didn't and six months later she had John at the free clinic. He was a premature baby, sure, less than five pounds, but he made it.

Compared to giving John up, doing a week of detox was nothing. She made several passes by the foster agency, even walking up the stairs once, John held tight in her hands, before she finally made it through the giant glass doors of the giant glass building.

But she did give him up and later, during one of her sober months, she tracked him down and found out a good family on the west side had adopted him and they were raising him as their own. Over the years she sporadically followed him as he played sports in high school, went to college and got a degree in engineering. She was proud of him, but she stayed away from him, too ashamed to do anything but watch him from a distance.

Until tonight.

"Hour's up," Numo said.

"Cripes, I can see de house up dere," she said. "Five minutes is all I ask. Please."

"Five minutes? Okay sure. That's it though. I'm not even giving you the chance to ask for more next time. The train needs to be moving on."

"What train?"

"It's a metaphor."

"What's...?"

"Never mind. You have your five. Now get."

Five was just enough to look in the window of the house on the west side where John was now raising his family. He had, she knew, three girls, all teenagers now. He had a wife who was beautiful by any man's standards. He had a house, two stories tall and wider than the whole mission building. And he had a beautiful front lawn, green even in the winter. She walked across, tip-toeing as if someone inside might hear.

In the window she saw him, so tall, such a man, standing at the foot of a spiral staircase, staring upward, his back to Gretta's window. He wore a dark suit and dark shoes and his hair was cut short against his head.

His wife soon swept down the steps and into his arms wearing a baby blue, sleeveless, satin dress that came only to her knees. He draped a giant fur coat around her that covered even her feet and led her towards the front door.

She saw him reach for the front door, saw light seeping into the night as he opened it, a fierce brightness that seemed to sweep everything away within it.

"Tanks for dat, anyway, Numo," she said.

"No problem sugar. Let's go take care of that cough," said her reaper, pneumonia, as he led her away.

CHAPTER TEN – WALK INTO THE HILLS

My father once wrote me a poem about walking into the hills and experiencing nature to get closer to spirituality. I still have it, written on a little white pad of paper he used to keep beside his chair. I didn't know he was a poet before the gift, and never saw him write poetry afterwards. So it was special. I must have been lost and he wanted to show me the way, show me how to become a man.

The boy woke on his thirteenth birthday from a violent nightmare full of blackness and blood. No light crept into his hut so he knew the sun still waited behind the mountains. He wiped a splash of sweat off his brow and took a shaking breath, lifting himself from the straw mat where he would never again rest his head.

He walked out of his hut naked and relieved himself at the bank of the Swift River, racing with the icy waters off the highest peaks of the Making Ridge. The village was quiet, all the huts cloaked in the light mist of the cool morning air.

He wanted to scream, to release the terror of his dream and anguish of the day.

He thought of his brother, the boy his brother once was. He remembered his laughter, haughty and jumpy like a grasshopper, as he ran along the river, their river, chasing the days to their end. That was two years ago. He hadn't seen his brother since. The boy knew it was the way, as it had always been. And then, two years ago, after his brother was no longer his brother, the dream found its way into the boy's nights.

It begins the same with the boy walking along a nearly forgotten trail, probably a trail where deer once climbed to the cool waters of the freshest springs on the mountains, or skipped down to the deep green grasses of the plains. At first the dream moves along sweetly. He can hear the river close to his left and smell its coolness. He can feel the wet clover under his toes as he strides proudly up the hill that leads to the Making Ridge. But the river soon goes quiet. The boy tries to find it again, but it's as if it never was. He gives up and goes back to the trail, which has also vanished. He's now in the middle of a black forest, the canopy overhead as thick as death and black as night. The floor is covered with dead, rotting leaves he's afraid to touch with his bare feet. And he's suddenly shivering cold. The boy gets his bearings the best he can and trudges forward, heading uphill in the hopes that he'll come out from under the evil forest and see light again, or at least hear the river's rush. But there are no sounds here, no animals singing or growling. Even his steps betray him to no one because the dead leaves are slimy with the dank life of decay. But they know he is coming, feel his difference, his vitality standing out like a scream in the middle of the night. And he can feel them as well; feel their loss, their sorrow and their hunger. Despite his training and the words of his father and his elders, he wants to run. If he runs, he will die. He knows this, but his legs shake with the desire to push forward, to dash through the forest and around the black, muck-covered tree trunks, until he found some light at the top, where he must go. If he could just run for a moment, take off and get away from this place, a place he knows surrounded by the others. He feels their eyes on him, watching him, spitting and voracious. Just a moment, I will run, he thinks. And so he does. And almost the second he starts forward, they are after him. He runs with every bit of his strength, desperate to get away from their grasp, feeling the dirty, pointed nails of one of them dig into his right arm. He pulls it free, but not before it rips a jagged line through him, his own blood spilling onto the putrid ground, feeding it. He tries to call his brother's name, but cannot speak. He tries to run faster to escape the evil behind him, but his feet are now slipping on the increasing slope of the hillside. He's moving backwards. He looks and sees a sea of red eyes and open mouths and reaching claws with dirty, pointed nails. As they pounce on him he wakes up, always at the point before he is consumed.

The best thing about his birthday was, one way or another, he was free of that dream. Because after today he would see the truth for himself. And horror or no, end or beginning, the dream would have no more to give him.

"Put on your cloth boy," the voice of his father came from the shadow of a willow hanging thirsty over the icy waters of the Swift River. "The rest will be up soon and you don't need to be showing that to the world."

"Don't call me boy," the boy said, trying to stare into the shadow and see his father's look of shock and anger. Instead he was rewarded with the old man's soft laughter.

"Son, I will call you man when it is time to call you man, and never before." They stood staring at each other for several moments, neither really able to see the other. The boy did not look away, even though he was painfully aware that his father could literally throw him halfway across the Swift with hardly a flick of his wrist. The silence had become uncomfortable and the boy thought he knew why.

"I will not be lost," he said to his father, trying to sound certain with his little boy voice. "I will come home, Father. I promise."

His father did not answer. Instead he broke from the willow's shadow, which had grown more and more defined with each moment the sun climbed up the backside of the mountains. As he walked away from his only son, the old man said, "You are the weaker of the two. But I don't think my body can take the loss, weaker or not. And your mother will wail like a banshee for thirty days and nights."

As was his father's way, he slipped, silently away as if the ground and quietly swallowed him whole.

Later that morning, during his feast, the boy ate until his stomach hurt. He had thought he would be unable to eat from the fear in his gut. But as soon as he smelled the roasting fowl and saw the colorful dishes of fruit and leaf prepared in his honor he could not help himself. It would be the only thing he ate until he did or did not return from Making Ridge. He ate so much his stomach had barely recovered before it was time to leave.

The sun had almost reached its highest point, high for the season of his birth, which was lower than his brother's summer sun. The boy was the weaker, younger child, but he would take the walk of Man Making and see what there was to see and return with the wisdom and power of a leader - after the sun rode the sky fifteen times over his adventure - so that his father might rest his final days. He would face his nightmare, if that be what sought him. He would face worse if worse were there. No boy knew what a man knew through telling. Boys knew when they became men. It was the most sacred knowledge of their village and of all the villages up and down the Swift. And the boy saw fear and sadness both in his parents' eyes as he stepped to the edge of the village, followed by all who could walk, so that they could take the first five steps of the man's journey together and the boy would know over those fifteen days, that he was not alone.

His mother kissed the soft palm of her own hand and placed it on his cheek.

"Be safe, my son," she said, smiling. "I will see you soon. Walk into the hills, my son."

The boy turned and walked from his village. The people he had known and grown with for the past thirteen years took the first five steps with him. The rest of the steps were his alone. As he followed the Swift upstream he heard his mother sobbing quietly.

The first day of walking was much like any walk or hike he had taken as a child. In fact, he had been over the shores of the river many times. He passed villages he had visited, even waved to some of those out enjoying the day. They didn't wave back. If they interfered in any way, even with a word or a gesture of encouragement, then his trek would be soiled and he could not consider himself a man. The boy knew this, of course, and signaled to them out of habit and loneliness, forgetting for a moment his journey.

By the end of the day, the boy had left familiar land and started up the gentle slopes that would become the steep climbs of the ridge. By his account, it would take three days to reach the sacred place atop the highest peak of the ridge and three more days back down. So he would need to spend nine days atop the barren rock with barely water to sustain him before tumbling back down the mountain to join his village as a man.

He was pleasantly surprised that sunset didn't bring on a host of ghoulish creatures and rotting plants. In fact, the land was quite tame as he walked through the night, resting under a large, leafed oak for a couple of hours just before dawn. He fingered his small knife as he walked, to be sure. But nothing real or beyond nature threatened him.

And so the days and nights went, not a soul save varmints, not a sound save the river and the cool wind through the trees.

He had misjudged the distance of the ridge by a day, so he didn't reach the foot of the final climb of the rocky terrain of the Making Ridge until the beginning of day five, which suited him fine. He would simply climb up the last, open expanse, wait out the hunger that already gnawed at him, drink what water he could find and then come back down.

By midday he was less than a stone's throw from the summit.

By later afternoon he reached the highest point of Making Ridge. He pulled himself up onto a flat slate, gasping in the thin air, weak from the lack of food. He looked about. The ridge seemed to go on forever north and south. To the west, looking into the sun, he could see where the river ran, but no village was visible.

And to the east.

The boy nearly fell off the ridge when he turned around again and saw a wild man standing not two steps from him, his gleaming, insane grin and wild eyes coming towards the boy, the lunatic's arms open to take the boy to unimaginable horrors.

The boy had no time to grab his knife, which was a good thing; because there was a very small chance he could have killed his only brother.

"Brother! I've been waiting for you," the crazy man, the boy's brother, yelled, his voice echoing down the ridge. "I knew your birthday and the day you would be here, but I guessed poorly and I was a few days early. But I wanted to be the one of us to come and greet you and invite you."

"Invite me? To where, insanity? Certain death? Are you dead big brother?"

His brother laughed a loud grasshopper laugh.

"Neither," the brother said, still giggling. "Let me show you."

And so that was how the little brother found out about the villages on the other side of the ridge, and how they sent their girls up the mountain to become women. He also found out about a third people, who lived on the ridge. They were the ones from both villages who decided to live elsewhere from their parents and make their own lives. His brother made that choice two years before and lived a happy life with a woman. She insisted the boy call her sister.

And even though the boy left his brother and his new sister to their new lives and returned to his own village as a man, he respected his brother for his courage to step outside of his world and pursue something utterly unknown.

And he died many long years later with that secret in his heart, leaving his sons and grandsons and great grandsons to find out the truth about Making Ridge.

CHAPTER ELEVEN – TRIVIAL PURSUIT

It was a major part of my young adulthood. The family would gather for the game, one or two sisters and their mates, my father, some family friends and me. I was not quite as worldly as the rest, being the youngest, but sometimes I got the science questions correct so they let me stick around. Those nasty little colored pie shapes were like gold in our home, coveted pieces of plastic the players would do anything to obtain. Some of the fiercest arguments in our house were over questions in Trivial Pursuit.

And my father always sat at the helm of team number one.

Dad was smart and possessed an almost supernatural need to know. I can still see his face getting more and more red, his voice growing louder and louder as he asserted his will and fought for victory over that piece of the pie. Unfortunately for my dad, brother-in-law number two also had the same drive to win, the same exceptional intelligence and the same need to know. So when the two played team captain, and they always did, a debate was inevitable.

Whatever the genetic makeup that causes that trait, it landed in me. Learning, to me, has always sat at the pinnacle of my lifelong motivation.

Well, that and sex.

And I'm not referring necessarily to high school and college and classroom, lecture, book, method learning. What greases the gears of life is knowing, and however that knowing manifests, whatever process works best for the individual brain, should be done.

In every job I've ever had I made myself the go-to guy. In every social situation I wanted to be the smartest person in the room. I want to know more than my kids and as much as my mate. I want my customers to tell business associates they learned this and that from me.

It's all vanity, I suppose, but it doesn't matter. When a characteristic is so deeply ingrained in a person's makeup, fighting it doesn't make sense. One of my teachers once told me that every person wants to be desired, to feel needed. If you don't feel a sense of self-worth, then you'd better change the scene. I never forgot that. It has become one of my credos, and I'll always feel a debt to that woman for that single day, for that one comment.

Another result of this attribute is the tendency to pretend to know when I truly have no idea. The older I get, the less likely I am to play that game, but my first decade as an adult was wrought with baseless assertions. To all of those who were misinformed by my convincing arguments free of any basis on fact, I am truly sorry. (See Chapter 7.)

By the way, I'm not really sorry. But I'm at least a little sorry that I'm not sorry so that should stand for something.

Whether a trivial pursuit or a worthy endeavor, the journey, the quest is what makes us who we are.

"We're going to get it today," the old man said as he pulled the rifle out of the tall, hardwood case, its glass revealing a row of other firearms all designed for the demise of various fauna.

The boy behind him nodded, though the old man couldn't see him, seemingly too engrossed in the gun in his thick, worn hands.

The dim room smelled of apples and wood polish and slight decay, heavy dark-brown curtains blocking the early morning sun, the insistent light piercing like a laser through tiny gaps at the window's edges.

The old man pulled a second weapon from the case and shut it, turned and pushed it towards the boy with a three-toothed smile. The boy's hands were in the pockets of his hooded sweatshirt and he made no move to grab it.

"Henry, this one is yours," he said. After a long breath, he wrapped his small hands around the barrel and looked at the weapon. With its butt on the worn carpet, it stood nearly his height. He could hardly lift it, hardly fathom actually raising its business end and pulling the giant trigger. He thought it would explode in his hands, knock him down, blow off half his face. He hated it instantly.

The old man was unaware.

"My name is not Henry," the boy said. "It's Hank."

The old man frowned.

"You aware where you got that name?"

The boy knew.

"You," he said.

"That's right, that's right. Henry is my name. Even though you call me Granddad. My name is Henry. You know how many people called me Hank? Do you?"

"No," the boy admitted, looking at his grandfather's feet, at the dirt on his giant boots, boots that looked like they were older than the boy. He avoided looking straight at his grandfather simply because he didn't like staring at his giant belly pushing against the red and black flannel shirt, seemingly the only shirt he owned.

"Not one. So you're Henry. If you don't like it, that's some tough shit for you. You're here to be a man, and Henry is a man's name."

Henry didn't argue, and soon they were on their way into the woods in a gray and red truck that squeaked and bounced down the narrow dirty road, leaving a giant cloud of dirt in its wake. He couldn't imagine any animal dumb enough not to see that cloud. He hoped they all saw it and ran for the hills.

Unfortunately for the boy and for the animals, after an hour of jostling and squeaking, the truck came to an abrupt halt in front of a thick stand of trees and the two got out and began hiking into the deeper woods of the foothills near the old man's home. The original Henry lowered himself to the ground and announced they had a long hike ahead of them. He produced a can of beer from somewhere under his seat, popped the cap and drank its contents in one long draught. He crushed the can with his big hands and threw the empty into the back of the truck.

After a long, deep, gurgling burp he said, "Let's go get us some dinner."

The boy followed the old man into the forest and up a hill. The sun now beat down heartily on the two, causing the boy to sweat and the old man to pant. The air seemed heavy, like the life of the plants and trees had escaped and was running thick into the boy's lungs. His hands got wet and slick and he feared his gun, now heavy and hot, would slip to the ground and go off, killing him instantly.

"You... tell me if you see anything," the old man said between heavy breaths.

The boy realized at that point he didn't even know what they were hunting. Deer? Duck? Bear? Alligator? Zizzer Zazzer Zuzz? He had no idea and thought asking at this point would make him look stupid. So he decided to just wait and deal with the seeing of an animal when he came to it.

They never found any animal to shoot, which would have made the boy happy if he weren't so very sad.

At the crest of a steep hill Henry's grandpa found a large boulder, sat down on it, hard, with an oomph and patted at his red, sweaty, fat neck with a dirty kerchief.

"Take a break," he gasped. There was no other rock, so the boy leaned against a scant tree, so devoid of any branches or leaves he wasn't sure what it was.

Henry looked out over the expanse of forest and mountains, feeling the heat dry the sweat on his skin. He squinted into the sun, and thought about the animals. Where were they? Probably sitting in the shade, finding some water somewhere or possibly looking at him right now, laughing at the loud, clumsy humans who thought they would catch them unaware to shoot them in the head, cut out their guts and haul the rest home to fry up with some fresh eggs and hash browns.

The boy heard a strange squeak behind him and turned around just in time to see his grandfather fall to the ground, clutching his left shoulder with his right arm, his face in a frozen grimace of pain, eyes clasped shut.

"Granddad?" he said. His gun slid to the ground and he

walked halfway over to his mother's father, found his feet wouldn't move another step, another inch.

"Damn," the old man said. "Damn heart."

"Granddad?"

"Get... help... now..." the old man said. "Go."

The boy ran.

It took him most of the day to find the road and the old, rusty truck and run the length of the dusty road back to his grandpa's house. He had to break the great big, front window of his granddad's house to get inside and get to the phone.

It was nearly dark when the men reached his grandfather and nearly midnight when they returned with his body to the old home with the old, heavy drapes. The boy sat inside by himself, on the old man's rocking chair, hugging a small pillow that smelled like the old man and apples.

A tired-looking man in a white uniform with a silver badge came into the house after knocking quietly.

"Son, are you in here?" he said.

"Yeah," Henry said.

"Son, I'm sorry..."

"I know," the boy said. "My parents will be back from their trip in the morning. I'll be okay till then."

"You're going to stay here by yourself?"

The boy looked up at him then, staring at him as hard as he could.

"Yes," he said.

"I'll ask the chief," the man said after a time. "My name is Stan. What's yours?"

"Henry," the boy said.

"People must call you Hank, eh?"

"Henry," he said again. "Hank is a little boy's name."

CHAPTER TWELVE - BELIEVE

I loved my grandfather and miss him very much. Both he and my grandmother were important parts of my life, especially as a young child. He was a sweet man, if not a little gruff and my parents honored him by giving me his first name as my middle name. I continued custom by giving my youngest son my father's first name as his middle. I hope he does the same for me. Traditions are rare commodities and I realize, as I get older, it is my responsibility to either rekindle those forgotten or create something new to pass on to my children. They are the anchors, after all, that can give us feelings of safety, security and family. And anytime that can be accomplished, the world doesn't seem so cold.

What did that story have to do with Trivial Pursuit? Very little. Except that the boy thought the hunting trip was trivial and instead it changed his life and how he thought about his grandfather. Unfortunately, as is often the case, he learned his lesson too late. But even through the tragedy, one can see the boy is stronger, more developed as a human being and feels more a man and less a child.

Looking back over these chapters so far, I see I'm showing a duality when it comes to belief and cynicism. Both are a part of my personality, may possibly be part of all of us. No one wants to be the chump, but most people probably would like to believe in something beyond what they can see, hear, taste, touch and smell. My father had this trait. One minute he'd be telling me the world was full of scams and swindlers. The next he'd be telling me the story of when he saw a UFO. And he told the story with such fire in his eyes and such unbreakable confidence and conviction, that I believed it then and still do. (See Chapter 7)

The night sky in the mountains is quite different from what can be seen from the city. It almost looks like a galaxy-sized Christmas tree with a billion strands of white lights. One can watch the various satellites trudge slowly east to west across the sky. Shooting stars look like falling comets, the Milky Way actually appears milky and the moon is a spotlight shining down, the strange face of a man hidden within its circumference. Everything is clear and defined and it seems to go on forever, which I suppose it does.

In his story he talks about a small group of disc-shaped lights that appeared over the mountain range to the east one night while he was sitting outside, having a beer with my grandfather and my mother's cousin. They all watched as the lights moved into the center of the sky, nearly over their heads, silently and impossibly fast. My father, who has been in love with aviation his whole life (Chapters 14 and 15) and would have been a pilot had his color-blindness not stopped him, estimated the speed of the crafts would have killed a man, especially when they turned, in perfect formation, ninety degrees to take off in another direction without slowing at all.

After several minutes of these maneuvers, the lights abruptly shot north and disappeared over the hills.

Did he make this up? I have no idea. The séance I mentioned in Chapter 7 actually happened with sister number three. And sister number four convinced me completely, one night, that she was the tooth fairy, which for some reason scared the holy hell out of me.

Whatever the reality, it may be unimportant.

And though it's been thought about and written about and told about a million times, here's a bit of a take from me and what could possibly be out there.

I am now certain I'm losing my mind. It's quite possible insanity now touches the majority of the children. I became aware of our mutual dementia last night – night is a relative term in eternal darkness – with the death of LK-2810.

He had taken the overnight shift at the observatory for the twenty-seventh consecutive time. His obsession with scoping had overtaken all else. Many of us have experienced the voyeuristic thrill of scoping and spent possibly more time than was healthy alone on the monitors. But anything over six or seven days is considered impolite. I found him the next day, his face burnt, his eyes gone, his mouth open in a statue's scream. The suicide was a desperate act of a despondent soul. And we all understood.

More than a few of us considered, for a moment, joining him.

There are thirty thousand children now. We have been told that there will be no more. My theory is that the parents decided any more than a ratio of six to one would cause them to lose control. They number about five thousand, though we rarely see them anymore.

The parents are quite mad.

When they first arrived, and the disappointment of their failure filled them, I can imagine the strength it must have taken to continue. They could not leave because their resources were spent and irreplaceable. And they could not stay because their destination was occupied.

The violence you find so common and so easy was simply not a genetic possibility for the parents. And the environment proved mortal to them anyway, so even if they had the will to destroy, it would have been senseless. So they accepted their doom of darkness and cold and no hope for anything more and set about the task of creating us.

The creation was not easy, and my apologies go to the thirty percent or so immune to the memory scrub. You're recollection of the necessary experiments was not planned and nearly caused the parents to abort. As I said, violence is not in their blood. But only a genetic infusion from you would ensure our survival.

It has been nearly one hundred years now since the parents first woke from their long sleep. Our lives extend much further than yours but they were grown at the beginning of their journey. They age and their minds become weak and soon they will die. Time is short.

We have been given, with your genetic code, the ability to survive on your world. With that has also come human tendencies. I have fallen in love with NC-2384. We love passionately as you do, full of lust and desire. We also have run the appropriate tests and found we have the ability to procreate much the way you do, which is our wish. Many of us have mated and wish to have offspring, but we would no sooner subject a child to these conditions than we would fly into the sun.

So our only option is Earth. But you have shown through your media how you view us. We are fodder for horror stories and tragedies and none of us believe you would allow us to coexist among you in peace. As a species you can barely stand your own kind if they have different skin or different eyes or hold slightly different beliefs. Trying to accept us would be like a bovine or swine standing up on its hind legs and asking to be invited to dinner.

But we will not stay where we are.

You have one week from the moment you receive this to evacuate all of Australia. In one hundred and sixty-eight hours we will eradicate all human life left on the continent. We have spent the past five years creating weapons sufficient to complete the task. We considered Antarctica because of the nearly non-existent human population, but the climate is too harsh. We would not survive. The dry, barren expanse of Australia suits us better.

In a handful of hours, one thousand of us will descend on our parents and kill them all. They would not let us go through with our plans being the docile creatures that they are. They would restrain us and rather let us die in darkness of old age and misery. Their insanity and frailty has brought them to the end of their lives anyway and their end is a benevolence. They will not even fight us as we strike them down.

You see, our parents cannot perform a violent act, are incapable of even considering the concept of brutality. But we have your chemistry and some of us, me included, enjoy the thought of violence almost as much as the thought of a sexual encounter. I was the first of us to kill. LK-2810 died easily at my hands and the thrill overwhelmed me. He did not commit suicide, but I am scrambling this part of the communication so that my own kind will not ever know it. He was weak and would not have contributed to our cause. And I am to lead my kind in our new hope, our new beginning, our long-awaited life.

We will populate the continent under the protection of a field strong enough to repel any retaliation from you. Let me be clear, because I'd hate for more humans to die than absolutely necessary. If you drop an atomic bomb on the force field, all of the radiation, all of the impact of the explosion will be felt by you and not by us. The fallout alone will kill several hundred thousand of your kind on the islands surrounding our new home.

We have some debate on what you will do with this information. I am the most hopeful, along with NC-2384. We think you will do what you must to save your own. But many of us think you will ignore our ultimatum and launch against us. Some think you must be given an example of our power before you do what we command, that we must kill some of you in order not to have to kill millions of you. Our taking of the continent will not be a battle. We will kill the remaining Australians from where we now are. You have no chance of affecting us in time, even if you had adequate weapons, which you do not.

You are all receiving this message either by radio, television or Internet communication. Those without such means, such as the Aborigines, are at your mercy.

And you are at ours.

CHAPTER THIRTEEN – TRAIN SET

Most men will probably tell you they wanted a train set as a boy. I was one of the few who, at seven years old, received the ultimate. It was one of the smaller scales, H-0 I think, with a nice long engine, yellow with a thin red stripe down the side, open and closed cargo cars, a whole string of them, and an old fashioned red caboose. The track circled twice around a four foot by six foot piece of plywood which had been decorated with little trees, a little town with a little train station, a hand-painted tunnel made from an oatmeal tube and handmade bridge. Everywhere were little people and little cars and trucks. The track had been laid down with perfect meticulous precision amidst a tiny, false countryside.

And the whole thing folded on hinges up against the wall, two shiny chains bolted to the ceiling holding it in mid-air for play.

My father built the whole thing. He loved building and this project was one of his finest. I had no idea what I was getting that year for my birthday, and I'm fairly certain I hadn't asked for a train. But there it was, a boy's perfect miniature fantasy.

And there was my dad; smiling that wide, crinkly, wet smile of his at the creation he had built for me... in his room.

Most dads must do that. I know I have. Dad buys something for his boy's birthday or maybe for Christmas that he's going to love, when in reality Dad just wants to play with the damn thing.

I cherished that train set and would love to have it today. But that present wasn't for me. I was the excuse to build something he couldn't have growing up a child in the poorest period in this country's history. I was the lucky kid who happened to be standing there.

I'm standing at the edge of Morris Pond, its glassy surface broken by a cluster of lily pads and the eyes of creatures waiting beneath. My five-year-old hands are digging for the magic rock.

The man who would wield the gem stands beside me, brown eyes glittering, worn teeth showing through full gray beard. He is my own personal Santa Claus.

"This one?" I ask, holding up a flat, black stone, white veins trailing over its surface.

The man appraises it; turning it in his giant, gentle hands.

"This. This is perfect," he says.

"Throw it. Throw it." I take a gulp of the root beer, the carbonation burning my throat, watering my eyes.

He stands ready, surveying the murky waters, gauging the distance and feeling the shape of the rock nestled between finger and thumb.

I woke the morning of the Lume, the dream fading, my cheeks damp with root beer tears.

"Damn," I said, wiping my face. I rose from the too-small bed of my tiny dorm, cluttered with unclean clothes, unfinished papers and uneaten stale fast food. My phone was singing to me. I rescued it from the floor.

"Answer," I said.

The disembodied head of my sister materialized above the phone. Her new little-boy haircut made her look like my twin with the same straight flat mop, same bright blue eyes and even the mess of freckles floating over her cheeks. I knew she was pissed before she opened her mouth.

"Where the hell have you been?"

My stomach sank as I remembered.

"Oh, crap Danielle. I'm sorry. I'll be right there."

I disconnected before she could say anything more.

I jumped on the transway and raced to her apartment on the other side of town. The car complained twice about my speed, but I ignored it, knowing I'd probably get a bill for the transgression.

As I pulled into the complex – a dozen low, white buildings circled around a parking lot, laundry and wet park – Danielle came flying out, short hair flipping wildly.

I jumped out and she was already yelling.

"You want to get me fired?" Despite her rage, her voice lilted across the parking lot, almost singing the words.

"You think this is funny, mister? I'm going to lose my job. Then guess what?" She pointed a short finger at me. "You get kicked out of college and I get kicked out of here.

"I'm sorry, Sis. Really. I just woke up." I tried a smile, meeting her halfway to her door and wrapping her in a forceful hug.

"Knock it off!" She pushed me away. "You went to the new club last night. I can still smell it on you." She curled her nose in mock disgust.

"The Factory. Wild place. The holos are insane. Bunch of little blue guys running around dancing with the girls."

"That's sick."

"Surprisingly no," I said. She stepped back, assessing me. I hated it when she looked at me that way.

"Okay pervee," she smiled. "Guess I'll trust you with my daughter. Go take care of Ice. She's already had lunch. No treats. And watch Gaz, okay. I think he's starting to manipulate her. She's been getting into everything."

"That's not Gaz. That's being five. Go."

I walked past her without another word.

"Don't forget about the Lume tonight," she called.

"I'm not going, Danny. You can't make me."

"How can you *not* go?" Her voice sang sadly across my back. I faced her, trying to look stern.

"I don't have to. I went the first year. That was plenty."

"But it's for charity. Do you have any idea the money they've raised this year alone?"

"Do you?" I saw she didn't.

"Well, it's a lot. They're making real progress. And what about Dad?"

I thought about our father and the dream, the recurring dream I had a hundred times over the last year, the dream that never finished. I never got to see him skip the rock. It was all the cruelty I could handle. And the Lume completely ignored our mother who had passed five years earlier when her car's nav gave out on the transway and she launched into the stratosphere, tumbling a dozen times or more before reaching the hard earth below. She wasn't part of the Lume. No one would remember her tonight. No one but me.

"What about Mom?"

"That's not fair, Don."

"Neither is this," I said, turning again and bolting into her apartment.

Before I could get the door shut she yelled, "I bought you a ticket."

A twelve-inch unicorn met me in the entry. It pointed a rainbow-shaded horn at me and smiled with a human face.

"Hello Uncle Don," Gaz said. The creature had a boy's voice.

"Don't call me that." The face of the thing disturbed me. It was Ice's face, or nearly like it, imbued with her genetic code.

"I'm sorry Uncle Don," Gaz said, smiling at its own joke.

"Where's Ice?"

"Trying to finish her ice cream before you make it to the kitchen."

"You're not much of an accomplice."

I gave Gaz a hard kick to the head. As my foot passed through it, I saw the fist sized silver ball that was the real Gaz. The holo recovered, flinching in programmed pain.

"That wasn't nice, Uncle Don," it said with a voice close to mock tears.

"Go pound your horn," I said and rounded the corner.

I found Ice at the table, blue eyes wide, lips circled with creamy remnants of the bowl she hid poorly in her lap.

"You're late," she said, her voice a miniature melody of her mother's.

"You're a disaster." I dampened a towel and worked at her face.

"Why are you late?" she asked. "Mom was cussing."

"You should have heard her in high school," I said. "And none of your business."

"Was it a whore?" the little voice worked joyfully over the bad word.

I laughed, looking down at Gaz. "You teach her that?" Gaz stared sadly.

"I know stuff, Uncle Don," she said.

"Too much apparently," I put the towel down and kissed her cheek lightly.

"Are you coming to the Lume tonight?"

"No."

"How come?"

"Because it's not real, Ice. It's no more real than your little gizmo there."

I regretted saying it as soon as the words left my lips. She cried instantly, the way only little girls can. I swooped her out of her chair and hugged her as tightly as I dared.

"He's real," she said. "As real as you. And we're related."

"I'm sorry sweetie." No use. The tears streamed down her face, her little body shaking with subtle sobs.

"Come on," I pleaded.

After a moment she whispered something I couldn't hear. Even after she repeated it I wished I hadn't heard.

"Go to the Lume tonight?" she said a third time, facing me with a sorrow-racked face.

In a stadium in the center of the city we gathered to remember, each wielding the genetic code of a loved one who had passed the test. Dad passed it easily enough, a virulent cancer eating through his intestines with violent enthusiasm eighteen months earlier.

At the signal, we walked onto the field, the grass-like fibers actually two-inch conduits ending in nearly microscopic projectors. The three of us walked, among the other claim jumpers, finding a small space to call our own for the next fifteen minutes. Danielle hugged me. Ice hugged my leg.

"Thanks little brother," she said.

I squeezed my sister and patted Ice on the head.

"No sweat."

She pulled back and we formed a triangle around our patch of field. She pulled a small mirror-like disk from her pocket and dropped it between us.

An electric hum coursed through the air and the thousands in the crowd let out a collective gasp.

"Grandpa," Ice whispered as an old man wearing a flannel shirt and a full gray beard materialized. The image looked around, seemed to see me, and held out its hand.

I looked down as he opened his fingers.

My faith was restored when I saw, resting in his palm a flat, circular black rock with white veins traveling across its surface.

Three years later – nearly every type of cancer eradicated – the Lume was opened to everyone and Danielle and I got to see both our parents once again.

CHAPTER FOURTEEN – BALSA PLANE

I owe that story to the American Cancer Society. Each year, if you've been in a hole, they hold their Relay for Life in cities and towns across the country. Dozens, maybe hundreds of teams walk a track in relay for twenty-four hours. After the sun sets on the first day, they hold the Luminary to remember those who have died from cancer and honor those who have survived. The track is ringed with small, white lunch sacks. Inside each sack is a candle and outside is a message for that person honored or remembered. After all the candles are lit, they shut the stadium lights down.

Anyone touched by cancer in any way should experience this event. Walking the track, reading the messages, feeling the collective emotion, the sadness, the bravery, the humanity, will take your breath away.

Balsa wood is one of the lightest, softest, most pliable woods in creation. It grows in South America to about thirty meters and is covered with giant green leaves. It's one-third the density of ordinary wood and yet the genius scientists of the world have classified it as a hardwood. What? Yes, a hardwood. Apparently being hard is not a prerequisite of behind hardwood. As a child, I didn't know any of this. I only knew that my dad was building something with fragile strips of wood and a delicate roll of white tissue paper.

He set up a card table in his room and covered it with newspaper. Unreadable plans pinned to the wall, the sugary scent of Elmer's Glue permeating the air and razor-sharp Exacto knives lying within a child's reach, my father took almost a year to build his Balsa plane.

The patience. The discipline. The procrastination. That last one is the real reason it took a year. I have the same problem. Right now I have paint in my garage, have had paint in my garage for an entire year waiting to be stroked across my kitchen walls. When the contest is putting it off today, I beat him hands down.

Coupled with that lifelong postponement of nearly everything is the impatience of a child when a task is at hand. When a job is finally started, it must be finished as fast as humanly possible. It existed in my dad and lives in me, and in at least two of my four children. It doesn't make for a very productive life. But it is exciting.

My father finished his Balsa wood glider on a cool, windy autumn day when the leaves were just beginning to show their true colors and the sun seemed to be in a hurry to disappear for the night. The plane was beautiful, nearly as long as I was tall with huge wings and a grand, tall rudder. Nose to tail was covered with the tissue paper, the plane's skeleton just barely visible beneath the opaque surface. It looked like it might fly a hundred miles.

It didn't quite make the hundred.

In his excitement at finally completing his yearlong task, my father ran out into the front yard and further into the dirt driveway in front of our house. I chased after him, flushing with excitement, not really believing that the glider's maiden voyage was only moments away.

I think I mentioned in chapter eight that we lived off a four-lane highway, a major throughway for the big trucks, most carrying logs out of the mountains. It was a noisy place to grow up, chaos both inside and outside the house. I can still remember the near constant rumble of traffic a hundred and fifty feet from my living room window, an old, thin-paned window that literally rattled with each passing eighteen-wheeler. Falling asleep to that sound on a lazy Saturday afternoon was possibly the sweetest sleep of my whole life.

I came out on our porch, ran down our driveway and through our fence and my dad stood in the wind, the noise and chaos of the traffic bearing down on him. He suddenly looked twenty-four instead of fifty-four.

He looked briefly both ways across the lanes of asphalt and I realized he was going to throw it across the road to land in the neighbor's grassy field across the highway.

Good plan.

He reached back with his throwing arm holding the back of the plane, his left hand steadying the front and threw the glider forward with all he had, which was considerable. (My father's arms on his six-foot-four frame were always impressively muscular, a result of genetics, not exercise. I have the same arms and now my kids look at me in the same way I must have seen him.)

As he released the plane either a gust of wind hit it or its aerodynamics were not quite sound because it went straight down, hard, into our driveway and broke into at least three pieces.

There were a thousand perfect places within five miles to launch that glider on its first flight out. Even if it were a one-time deal and it was destined to sail off and never be found again, we could have found a fantastic place, high enough that we wouldn't even have to throw it, the grade of the mountain itself would give it the lift it needed.

That anxiousness, that palpable tension in the hands to get the task done, to start the deal, to fly the glider, was for him, and has always been for me, a double-edged blade. Sometimes you accomplish great things. But sometimes your glider never gets off the ground.

Born of inferior birth.

Elizabeth heard the phrase many times before the age of five, but never quite knew what it meant. She only knew the term had been applied to her and it seemed significant to the people who owned the house where her mummy worked.

They never said it in front of Elizabeth's mother, only when she wasn't there, had left her daughter to a snack in the kitchen or to play in the dusty, smelly stairwell, away from a party or important dinner going on at the other end of the house. And they didn't say it directly to Elizabeth, but would always glance at her as if they caught a bad scent after they said it.

Born of inferior birth.

The little girl wasn't bothered much by it. Her mummy had always told her some people were rude, even if they didn't know it, and it was their job, as polite women, to make up for inferior manners with their own grace.

Then, shortly after her fifth birthday, one she spent alone in her stairwell - she would never call it hers out loud, but she had come to think of the space as her own because she could hide little bits of string and pretty Autumn leaves and interesting rocks under the steps and no one would ever see them - the words gained meaning, sharp, heavy, bad-tasting meaning beyond rude, beyond manners and beyond Elizabeth's patience.

A young boy lived at the house, although Elizabeth rarely saw him. His name was Thomas-The-Third. She didn't know what that meant, but it sounded important because when people spoke of him they always say Thomas-The-Third. The two had never spoken to each other, but he stared wide-eyed at her whenever they passed in the great halls or he peeked her through a briefly open kitchen door as plates full of delicacy were being served.

He seemed a fat and awkward boy, as if his arms and legs moved about on their own, his worried eyes watching them go this way and that, afraid what they might do. He sometimes had trouble breathing as well, which is what happened the night the boy disappeared.

She had just left the kitchen, her Mummy alone and cleaning the fine china from a night of many, many guests, and was headed down the hall towards her stairwell when a strange noise up ahead in the shadow of the giant hall made her stop. She listened intently at the soft rasping noise that sounded like a sharp-toothed, long-tongued beast's breath as it sized up the little-girl meal before it. Had she not heard the boy make that sound in past months, she would have certainly screamed and ran back to her Mummy.

"Boy?" she called. He didn't answer. She stepped forward and called him again. After the third time and a few more steps she saw his pale form behind a small table that sat just outside one of the dozens of guest bedrooms of the house.

"Why didn't you answer me?" she asked. He still didn't answer, instead pointing to his throat, his mouth open as he took his little raspy breaths. "Oh," she said. She could see he was scared, even in the hall's dim light. He had a bit of sweat across his forehead and his hands were shaking.

Elizabeth knew what to do to help him. She had never been told, had never seen anyone treat him in any way. In fact when he would have a spell such as this, she would always be quickly ushered away.

She knelt in front of him, her knees pulling on her ratty dress and took his closest hand in both of hers, laying it flat between her palms and rubbing, slowly back and forth.

"It's okay boy," she said as softly, as calmly as she could. "Just breathe slow. It will go away soon."

Though the boy was bigger than Elizabeth she then wrapped her arms around him, scooting a little closer, and pulling her to him, rubbing his back very slowly and humming a tune her mummy always hummed to her at night when she couldn't sleep. His breathing eventually eased out of the attack and the rasp went away and after what seemed like several long minutes, he pulled away from her looking up at her as if she were a total stranger.

"Thank you," he whispered, smiling shyly.

And then everything went to the moon.

Someone, the girl later found out it was one of the eldest women of the house, grabbed her by the neck and pulled her away from the boy, into the air when she hung, flailing her arms and strangling. When she thought she might die from the pain or simply from not being able to breath, she was tossed against a wall, hitting her head hard and falling into a mess on the floor, the world spinning around her.

"Born of inferior birth." She heard it again and again in that hall. Only now no one was whispering anything. Women were screaming those words as loud as their old voices would allow. Then she heard her mummy's voice and was pulled into the air again, this time gently. She recognized the smell of her mother mixed with the soaps she used on the fine china, and fell against her bosom.

When she woke, maybe the next day, maybe several days later, she was back at the house she and her mum shared with twenty-seven other people. It was a large house, five or six bedrooms, but even in the girl's state, they weren't given the privacy of their own room while she recovered.

Her mummy cried when the girl awoke, and hugged her very tight, which hurt her shoulder but Elizabeth didn't complain because she thought it would be bad manners.

Eight years later, the girl was a young woman and she and her mum now lived in the house where her mum worked, owned by a kindly man and wife who lived more in the country and less in the city. Elizabeth had very nearly forgotten the night she helped the little boy. She worked alongside her mum now, earning her own board, her own room and sometimes a little extra for a treat in town.

On a dry, cold morning she was out in the garden, tending the turnips and rhubarb the old man said he liked more than anything in the world. A young boy rode up to the house on a large, black horse. He was near Elizabeth's age, maybe a little older. He had broad shoulders and fine, blond hair and rosy cheeks from a fast ride in the chill. He smiled when he saw her, as if he'd uncovered a buried treasure chest full of gold.

She didn't recognize him until he was close enough for her to hear his breath, stronger than the night in the hallway, of course, but still a bit raspy, a bit labored.

"Elizabeth," he said.

"Boy? Thomas-The-Third."

He hopped off his horse and walked over to her, leading the steed that took an interest in Elizabeth's turnips.

"Tom, please," he said and bowed in front of her. She stood from her gardening, staring at him.

"I'm fifteen, now," he said eventually. "I turned fifteen two weeks ago. I'm a man now. My father, who is getting so old and stupid, told me that I had to find someone to court and eventually to marry."

The girl flushed but still did not speak.

"I told him who I had loved since I was seven years old and

he almost died right in front of me." He laughed as he said this, as if he were a touch proud of himself.

"I told him if you wouldn't be my fiancée, then I would never marry and there would not be a Thomas-The-Fourth. I told him you saved my life and there was no other woman who had saved my life and I was in debt to you ever more."

Still she did not respond.

"I told him to mind his own apples and grapes."

"But, I can't..." he put up a finger to stop her.

"I know. I'm a lunatic. You cannot. But can we have a walk, then? At least that? I have spent two weeks tracking you down and most of my life thinking about you. Just a walk?"

He put out his hand and she took it, feeling the soft strength of his fingers.

They walked along the country road in the cool morning air.

CHAPTER FIFTEEN – KITE

For those of you trying to private eye the connection between my narration and each of the stories, please stop. Some of them go together and some of them do not. Still, come to think of it, if the connection is profound and you are going to credit me with that, then go right ahead.

My father's love of flight, I think, was also a genetic trait like the procrastination/impatient bug in Chapter 14. But this one missed me completely. My little brother, who didn't have our father's color-blindness, wanted to fly as much as Dad and made a career out of it in the Navy. Of all the wonderful things my dad's children have done in their lives, I think that one makes him the happiest. He wanted to fly so much; it's good that at least some of his genes get to sit in the cockpit.

While he walked this blue marble, my dad would often make use of kites to at least get something in the air. There was a windy mountain, really a mass of red cinder rock courtesy of one of the nearby volcanoes, that we would drive to and launch kites.

My most vivid memories are of the bat kites, the plastic triangle stunt kites that would whip back and forth, diving to the ground only to turn at the last moment and shoot back into the upper atmosphere. They had giant yellow eyes painted on the black plastic and they looked positively mischievous. We were so high up on this sharp incline that if our kites had any string out to speak of and the string broke, the kite was gone forever, tumbling down two or three hundred feet and out of sight. In fact, I think the rule was to fly the kites until there were no more kites to fly.

We also did the parachute men. It was so much fun to put a paper clip on the poor guy, fashion a shallow hook with an end and hang it on the kite string. The wind would work it up the length of the string and when the little plastic man reached the top and hit the kite in flight, it would drop and chute to the ground.

I'm not much of a kite flyer without my dad. Remember the genetic thing? My joy was in doing it with him. My children like to do nearly anything with their dad. It's amazing how mundane the activity can be and they just want to be there, helping, playing, sharing.

Although I don't always follow my own advice, let your kids help. They will outgrow the desire and leave you with regret if you don't take advantage now of how great they mistakenly think you are today.

He could fly.

He was young and weak compared to his parents and his brother, but he was honorable and would soon be stronger than all. He imagined reaching the highest skies of their valley, the great green expanse split by the cool, quick river full of fish and surrounded by the three, white-topped mountains. On the largest of the three mountains grew a tree older than his family's memory, because it had always been their home. The massive branches of the great, thick, twisted pine went on forever and the nest built near the top of the tree was so big he could get lost going from one end to the other.

And now he could fly.

At first he was terrified for it was a long way to the forest floor from the giant nest. His mother crowded him in the nest, slowly moving him closer to the edge, making his home smaller and smaller. But he was too young and scared and he scuttled around her ducking of to the far end of the nest, only to have her crowd him again.

But one early morning, just a few suns ago, he woke and his mother was already standing by him, nudging him, opening her wings so that he could not escape. He turned and his father was there as well, standing on a perch branch just off the nest, watching him, commanding him to take the air. And what could he do but try his wings and jump? He stumbled twice through the air, falling much quicker than he thought he could. But then, quite by themselves, his wings opened and he was gliding through the trees down the mountain and into the valley.

And he could fly.

He soon dove into the icy waters of the quick river and caught his first earned meal.

Before long he had flown over the entire valley, or most of it anyway, and even lifted a rabbit and carried it most of the way back to the nest. His weak wings couldn't make it up the mountain, but he took it far enough, and his father was proud when he swooped down and lifted his son's kill the rest of the way.

The day of his father's death, they had been flying together, his father showing him how to lift himself on the breeze and catch the higher currents. They had reached a goodly height when a sound split the sky. He heard his father scream once, short, and then his beautiful wings folded and he dropped as a stone to the valley floor.

He dove after him, hoping to catch him, but he was too slow and too weak to reach him and lift him. But he was close enough to see his father's head hit a large stone and his body bounce on the ground. His father was broken, gone.

He landed next to his father's empty body and called out long and hard to his mother and brother. But they were too far away and he knew they wouldn't hear.

Then the man things appeared. Two of them walked into the grove where his father had fallen. One, large and round with red and black feathers and holding a giant black stick, was squawking at the other. He didn't know what they said, but he could read a father's reprimand.

The smaller, also carrying a big stick, seemed ashamed.

"Come on Joe," the big one said. "We gotta see if you killed it. I won't let that eagle suffer. You gotta see what you did."

"Dad, no," the small one said. "I didn't know."

"Hell you didn't!" the big one squawked. "You know exactly

what you did. I don't know how you got him from that distance, but you knew it wasn't no pheasant. Damn it, Son, that was the bird not to kill, the one foul you just don't kill. Look, there he is."

He had hidden behind a bush, but couldn't bring himself to leave his father completely.

They circled his father, looking down at his ruined body.

"No, he's dead."

"I killed him?"

"Well, you got him. There it is right in his breast there. Caught him dead center. Drilled him. He would have died from that, but it was the drop that got him. Bashed his head against the rock, probably."

"Oh."

They were quiet for a while. He didn't know what to do. If he moved, they might finish him as well. If he didn't move, they might catch him just standing here, cowardly, behind the bush.

"Let's go then," the father man-thing said. "Nothing to be done."

They started off, but then the boy turned around and looked directly at him. He must have brushed a leaf with his feathers.

"Dad," he whispered, staring directly at him, into his eyes. "Dad."

"What is it?" The father turned and followed his son's gaze.

"I don't see any... oh wait. What is that?"

"It's another one. A baby. Maybe I shot its mom."

"No that's a male. Probably related though."

"What do we do?" They had both crouched low to the ground and looked at him, into his eyes. He wanted to flee, to take off into the sky, but he knew that these man-things had killed his father and they would kill him.

"Leave him there. He'll find his way home. Come on." The big one said, standing again and pulling the little one after him. They walked away, the little one looking over his shoulder all the while, waiting for him to do something. He stayed still.

"I'm sorry, baby bird," the little one called back. "I'm real sorry 'bout your dad."

Long after they were gone and he heard no more sounds in the forest, he finally left his hiding place and approached his fallen father. A light breeze blew across him and his feathers, now all a mess, moved slightly. The rest of him did not. He was gone. This was no longer his father.

He noticed the light dimming and took wing, circling once, twice then three times over the clearing as he climbed to find the air current that would let him glide home. In the sunless dusk he soon lost sight of the thing that was once his father. And then the breeze lifted him and he began soaring towards the mountainside.

As he rose up to his giant nest in the giant tree, he thought of his mother and his brother and wondered what made them whole and what his father's feathers and beak and claw had lost.

And that was his first thought of his own soul.

CHAPTER SIXTEEN – SEE THE GAMES

I liked that last story. I like the thought of certain animals having much more awareness than humans give them credit. Not while I'm eating a steak, of course, or a chicken breast or pork chops. That would be hypocritical. Just when I'm looking at the animals from afar and appreciating their place in nature.

My oldest son is a vegetarian because he's seen how animals that give us our meat are treated and he can't stomach it, literally. And this is a child who has always loved fast food burgers more than almost any other food. So he gave it all up and I admire him for his conviction. I wish I had that kind of strength. Maybe I do, but he shows his strength to the world and I love him for it.

My father went to my sister's games. This may seem like a minimal statement, except that my sister (sister number four) played every single sport known to women. She always seemed to be wearing a headband and sweats and coming from or going to some practice or another. And when the games were on, my dad was there, supporting his daughter and cheering her name.

I paid attention to that and have always tried to show the same attention to my kids. When my daughter is cheering for her high school, I sit in the stands and watch her hoot and holler and smile and jump and I'm so very proud of her. There are other parents, the saintly set, who actually coach those football teams and cheerleading squads, who teach dance and ballet and art and kung fu karate. Sister number four is one of those and, of course, all of her kids are in sports as well. I don't quite reach that level of parenting, content to sit on the sidelines and watch. Any team I tried to coach would take last place anyway, so why put the kids through that. And yes, that is a lame excuse, but I'm sticking with it.

Just last week, my wife and I went to an awards presentation at our first-grade daughter's school where she received a citizenship award. There was another girl there, who we know, who was looking for her mom the whole time. She finally found us and waved and smiled and we took a picture and she was happy. But she would have been so much happier had her mom made the time. I'm sure she was working and that sometimes it's not possible. Balancing four children's schedules is nearly impossible. But children don't forget and if it's possible to make the time, the time must be made.

My dad went to my sister's games, but I don't remember him coming to mine in the two years I buckled under peer pressure and played one terrible game of football. I wonder if he did. Maybe kids do forget after all.

Freddy's parents didn't believe him when he said there was an explosion in the basement furnace and now there was a catastrophic fire burning that would soon inflame the entire house. And who could blame them because they didn't have a basement and the smoke detectors hadn't beeped one single beep.

His mother waggled a finger at him when he told them he had taken all the candy from the grocery store check-out stand and that the police would soon be coming to pick him up and take him away for "who knows how many years!" She did so because she loved him and knew he hated chocolate and chewing gum and would never take a single piece from anyone, even if it were offered.

His father barely acknowledged him with a nod when he told him he had uncovered a dinosaur head from the backyard and it was probably the biggest find in archeological history. He went on to say that the heads of NASA were going to genetically recreate the dinosaur and that it would no doubt devour their entire block within the week. He tuned out his imaginative son because he had been listening to him say these types of things since he was four. The boy was now eight and that was a long time to hear an endless stream of stories existing solely in the boy's mind.

His teachers were especially bothered by his creativity. They said in every teacher's conference that the boy was a major disruption to the classroom and that he was taking away the teacher's time that would be better spent teaching the other students.

And so it went, his little life, as he told his stories and they all ignored him again and again and again. They treated him with disdain and indifference; they condescended him and were annoyed by him. They did everything to him except give one single story of his any credit or kudos or recognition at all. But he kept telling them because he had no choice. For him, the stories were part of breathing and to stop telling them was to suffocate.

One day, after school, Freddy was walking home, creating a terrific story of a snake that got into a little girl's sleeping bag. The little girl in his story bore a striking resemblance to a little girl in his class who had stuck her tongue at him at recess when he tried to tell her a different story altogether.

Anyway, this little girl - the one in the story - was consumed whole by the giant python, who lived off her for an entire year. The story was blossoming in his head as it always did, as the flowers were now blooming along the white fence in front of the house where he now walked.

He looked up at the house and nearly screamed when he noticed, as if she hadn't been there before, a very old woman with long, straggly white hair, standing in the shadow of the porch, which was heavy with the growth of vines. She stared at him with white eyes and when he saw her and jumped back, almost into the street, she moved forward out of the shadows and screamed a word at him he did not recognize. It sounded like "krakoratay."

He felt the firm hand of a passer-by on his shoulder push him back onto the sidewalk just as a bus flew by the house, its horn honking loudly.

He spun around and no one was there. The boy turned back and the woman had also disappeared.

"Hello?" Freddy said quietly. There was no answer.

Eventually, and because it was getting late and dark, Freddy went on home.

That night he tried his snake story out on his sister, who had no patience for it at all. He thought maybe it needed work, possibly could use a sinister snake master or maybe the girl could have a secret knife she uses to cut her way out of the beast. Or maybe there was another girl, or maybe the girl and snake could become one being and set about ravaging the countryside and scaring the entire neighborhood. Tucked away in his bed, so extremely excited about his new story, he could hardly sleep. But eventually sleep took him away and he rode his dreams into the night.

She waited there for him, the haggard old woman with the white eyes. He had almost forgotten her. But she stood there on the porch in his dream, her eyes grabbing him like a barbed whip and pulling him towards her.

"Oalipanosha," she hissed. "You will come to me tomorrow. Oalipanosha. Come to me before it is too late. Tomorrow."

The boy tried to move away from her, but her eyes held him.

"Oalipanosha," she said one last time, her voice winding down and burning away like a dying fire.

When Freddy woke that morning, the word was in his mind, clear as the new sun rising over the city's highest scrapers. He didn't tell any stories to his mother, father or sister that morning, his brain too full of the old woman in the vine-covered house behind the white fence.

He ate slim at breakfast and then walked the long way to school, avoiding the old woman's street altogether. As he got closer to school, the word she had uttered in his dream beat louder and louder in his head. Oalipanosha, Oalipanosha, Oalipanosha, her voice chanted over and over. By the time he sat down for class, the sound of the word was so loud he could not hear the teacher speak or the children giggle and play. He asked to go be excused to the bathroom and left the class before his teacher could respond, not that he would have heard.

He passed the bathroom in the hall and ran outside the front doors of the school, sprinting back towards home and towards the old woman with the white, tangled hair.

She was standing on her porch, exactly as the day before when he panted up to the house with the white picket fence. She wore a long, gray dress that moved in the slightest breeze.

"What do you want?" he asked immediately, the strange word easing out of his brain, letting him go.

"To talk child. Merely to talk. We have nearly run out of time. It is nearly too late."

Freddy put his arms across his chest.

"So talk."

The woman turned her white eyes up and down the street.

"Not here, child. You must come inside. There I can show you what you have done."

"No way," Freddy said shaking his head. Immediately, Oalipanosha popped back into his head. The wave of it almost put him on his knees.

"I'm afraid you have no choice child. I promise no more harm will come of you if you heed what I must tell you."

He nodded his head and the pressure again left him. He took a few deep breaths and then raised his eyes, surprised to see the woman standing at the gate of the white fence, holding it open.

"Come now."

Inside, the house was not as dark as he had imagined. White candles danced merrily in each room and yellowish lamps blazed in every corner. The walls were covered with giant paintings or tapestries or old black and white photographs. She led him through two rooms and into a kitchen, decorated much as any kitchen with pots and pans hanging on hooks overhead and a sign on the wall that read, "Kiss the Cook." He almost laughed at that.

She pulled out a metal chair for him, and went to the old, rounded refrigerator.

"I have cookies, Frederick," she said. "Chocolate chip is your favorite. And some chocolate milk to go along."

"Thanks," he said. "But you forced me to come here."

She pulled a tray from the refrigerator holding a plate of cookies and a tall glass of the promised chocolate milk. She put it in front of him.

"I will not apologize. What you have done is far worse and if you don't stop, if you don't start using your powers for the cause of good, you will become my enemy and the enemy of many others."

"Lady, I don't know what you're talking about. I haven't done anything. Okay, maybe I've done some stuff. But nothing to you or this house. What did I do to you?" He paused for a breath. "And how do you know my name?"

He grabbed one of the cookies and shoved it in the chocolate milk before slurping it, whole, into his mouth.

"Frederick," she said, sighing heavily. "You are a Teller. There are precious few left in the world, but you are one."

He pointed to her and raised his eyebrows.

"Me? No, not at all. I'm a witch sent by another witch to keep an eye on you, to collect your stories."

"Collect?"

"Yes here," she said and placed a ball of glass in front of him about the size of his head. She put both hands on it and said, "Yutunima." The glass ball instantly blazed with a million colors, all moving behind the glass, mixing and turning and swirling, filling the room with dark, fierce lights.

"Look," she said.

Freddy looked and saw, within the glass ball, every single story he had ever imagined. He even saw, when he had looked long enough, the four different versions of the snake-girl story he considered the night before. They were all there, in perfect, real pictures as if he had a gazillion dollars and had hired actors and computer graphics experts to make movies just for him. He was delighted.

"This is so cool."

The old woman laughed.

"Yes, Frederick. It is cool, as you say. But if you don't stop until you've been properly trained, every story you've told since you were able to tell will be unleashed upon the world."

He looked at her. "How can that be?"

"I will show you someday. But if you don't heed my words, when the crystal can no longer hold your powers, and that time is coming quickly, every story will come to be and many people will be hurt or killed."

"So what do I do?"

She put her finger up to her lips. "No more stories. You will visit me regularly and I will help you control yourself. Tellers can do great things to this world, can save many lives, can end wars, can stop disasters. There is very little end to what you might accomplish. And for the rest of my days - however long or short they may be - I am your servant. If you heed. Will you heed?"

The boy smiled, suddenly feeling at home for the first time in his life.

"I will heed witch," Freddy said.

CHAPTER SEVENTEEN – IN THE CLOSET

How come I didn't get a witch telling me I had special powers when I was eight years old? What a rip off. Freddy is way lucky, the little bastard. So many stories are about someone finding a magical strength within them and doing something heroic with that strength. It's a human fantasy, one we all share I think.

So I'm pretty sure I mentioned I liked to snoop around in my dad's bedroom when I was young. If not, it is a fact, a given, that I went through everything that man owned more than once. He had no secrets from me at all, but he also had nothing that interesting. I found not one single girly magazine. One time I found a half-gone bottle of vodka, but that was only once and at the time - as opposed to now - I didn't care for vodka. I love vodka now. I wonder if my dad's genetics had anything to do with that. Thanks for the alcoholism dad. I really appreciate it.

Well my dad had a big, walk-in closet, holding mountains of shoes and pants and ties and shirts. And I loved to go through his stuff.

One year, about two weeks before my birthday, I was snooping through his closet and found all my presents for the year. My dad did most of his shopping for me at Radio Shack. I had every 100-in-1-Experiments box they carried, several radio controlled cars, a microscope and a chemistry set carrying chemicals they probably don't put in chemistry sets anymore. He got them all from his favorite store, which for many years was mine as well.

There were a lot of presents in there, all for me. I was able to stare for hours at everything I was going to get, playing with each toy in my mind. Honestly I don't remember what they were. I just remember the thrill of finding them, of hitting that jackpot.

A few days after my discovery of the presents in my dad's closet, he did something unexpected. For the longest time I thought he did it because he couldn't stand to wait, much like me. But now I think he may have had something else in mind. You be the judge.

When no one else was around, he took me in his room and showed me all my presents. I had to act surprised in front of him and then act like I needed to act surprised in front of everyone else. Because although he was showing me my presents, I still had to wait until my birthday to unwrap the as-yet unwrapped gifts. It was very confusing and difficult to hold the deception clearly in my mind.

I always thought he revealed my gifts because he simply couldn't wait another day before showing me all the cool things he bought. But just recently a new thought has occurred to me, something closer to the sixty-dollar incident. (See Chapter 6) Maybe he was showing me because he had caught me already and he wanted to make me feel guilty for my snooping. He wanted to confront me, but couldn't directly, so instead he took me to the closet and watched me squirm around a bit. What do you think?

Jason grew up in a little town that gave no credence to homosexuality. That's not entirely true. The typical townie credited gays, fags, lesbians and dykes with most of the decent jokes running through the town bigot pipeline; niggers, spics and Jews taking a close second, third and fourth in the joke conglomerate. Jason laughed at the jokes and passed them along. He chided the more effeminate students at his high school. If a kid didn't play football, he was definitely gay. If a chick didn't have a steady boyfriend or, forbid, had short hair, she was positively a carpet-muncher. And in a small town, once some homo was found out, they might as well have had a bright pink neon sign over their head every waking moment until they graduated and could legally escape.

It was hard for them, Jason knew, but what could he do?

If he stuck up for anyone, "we" would become "they" and he would become one of them. He'd seen it happen, almost in a blink. All it took was one of the jocks, one of the royalty, one of the judges of the school, to decide he or she thought you might be a little limp in the wrist, light in the loafers, a fudge-packer or daisy-picker, and the deal was done. No trial, no hearing, no jury, nothing. Just you and your new nickname and a complete end to any sociality.

And the irony was that most with the label, weren't.

One boy - definitely in love with women but just as definitely a practitioner of good hygiene, wearer of uptown clothes purchased at least two hundred miles away and the best cook in the home economics class - got the worst branding Jason ever saw. After P.E. in the showers one afternoon, one of the jocks came running through the locker aisles, still wet and with a panicked look on his face. He was screaming in fear (but with a touch of a smile in the corner of his mouth) that Tom had a hard-on. It was the unequivocal sign that a person wanted to screw boys. Jason never actually saw the famed erection, but that boy's life was essentially over.

First, eighty-five percent of the student body teased him mercilessly. That went on for the rest of the week. Then, that Friday night, the jocks (Jason included) egged and TP'd his house. And the following night, they caught him coming out of the video store where he worked, and beat him. In the end he survived with one missing tooth, an eye almost swollen shut, two broken ribs and bruises covering most of his body. Jason missed the beating, but expressed grave disappointment at not making the festivities. Finally, two weeks before the end of his junior year, Tom downed the contents of a prescription bottle in his mother's medicine cabinet. It was half full of sleeping pills, the strong ones, and had it been two-thirds full he would have died.

Tom's family moved away that summer, taking Tom to a place where he could receive counseling. The jocks joked that they were going to try and get the fag off him. And the ruling bodies continued to look for new suspects.

It was during that summer that a tiny little switch in Jason's head flipped to the on position. Most of it probably came from what happened to Tom. But that was only a catalyst for a building tension within him and a growing distance between what he knew was right and what he said and did. His conscious powered up and he decided to make some changes.

As Jason's senior year kicked off and the cruelest of the boys began to descend, especially, on the freshmen, Jason stood back. First he didn't laugh at the jokes. That wasn't hard because he never once thought any of them were funny. The joke-tellers looked at him quizzically, but Jason just shrugged and walked away. Then, bolstered by a first step completed, he moved on to the second phase of his plan.

Sitting at lunch with the other football players about two weeks into school, the quarterback started throwing peas at known fag and cocksucker, Bryan Donovan, two tables over. Bryan ignored him, so the other players joined in the barrage of overcooked legumes.

Willing his body, pushing with all his mental might, Jason stood up from the table, took his tray and moved to a different, mostly empty table, across the hall. He felt the eyes on his back, but no one spoke and no peas came his way.

For the third phase, Jason would actually have to open his mouth.

It didn't take long for an opportunity to arise. Apparently the meanest of the mean hadn't anyone to harass all summer and had some serious make-up work due.

It was rumored that Bryan Donovan flipped Scott Winslow the bird during lunch. No mention was made within the rumor about the two hundred or so peas that splattered all over Bryan and his clothes. In Jason's high school, a middle finger was as good as a bullhorn invitation to fight. And so, the rumor went on, there would be one, right after school, in the woods behind the gym.

Jason knew Bryan wouldn't show, had probably found out about the alleged fight around the same time Jason did. If Bryan had a modicum of intelligence, which Jason knew he did after their Calculus class together the year before, he would be running, full-board, in the opposite direction as soon as the final bell rang. So the jocks would be mulling around in the woods after school, a tentative crowd watching for Bryan and the teachers wisely staying clear of the whole situation.

That was Jason's chance. It would get worse for Bryan after today, so Jason had to move now.

As Jason approached the scene, he realized he had mistakenly translated Bryan's book smarts to common sense. He had visualized the scene almost perfectly, save that in the middle of the growing crowd stood Scott and Bryan, not a ruler between their noses, each bracing for the inevitable impact to come.

Jason walked through the sea of lettermen jackets and up behind his quarterback.

"Scott," he said loud enough for everyone to hear. Scott didn't take his eyes of his adversary.

"What," he said. "I'm busy. I'm about to cut a hole through this fag in front of me here. I can smell the dick on his breath."

"He's not gay," Jason said.

"What do you know?"

"I know he's not gay." Scott turned and eyed Jason.

"How? I saw him sucking dick the other day."

"No you didn't."

"Hey, I don't need you to..." Bryan tried to cut in, but Jason stopped him.

"Bryan this isn't about you, so just pipe down, all right."

"Listen Scott. About ten percent of the world is homosexual. And ninety-percent of those people are smarter than you. You know why? Because you wouldn't know one if he was standing right in front of you. You wouldn't get it if he was your best halfback. You wouldn't understand if he was your bud since kindergarten." Scott's eyes bugged as his slow mind put together the obvious clues Jason was throwing. "Ten percent Scott. That means if we have twenty guys on our football team, there's a good chance that two of them are gay. That's me, in case you hadn't figured that out, and one other guy."

Jason smiled.

"Would you like me to tell everyone who the other guy is?"

Scott didn't move or speak for several moments. The crowd seemed to hang on the silence, motionless, the reality of what they were seeing dawning on each of them, individually, in their own time.

"Go to hell," he finally said and pushed through the crowd, his football toadies unsure of what to do.

CHAPTER EIGHTEEN – GOLFING WITH DAD

Any of these surprising you? I didn't see the end of that one coming. The whole story comes from when I played football in high school and during a pre-game party at a couch's house a paper was distributed to all the boys containing at least fifty or sixty black, Mexican and homosexual jokes. At the time I thought it was funny. But that's how brainwashing works. When it's happening you don't know it's happening. If I had the presence of mind to think about the jokes, really consider what they were about, I don't think I would have had the courage to speak against them.

I hit my first golf ball three years and five months ago. That's about thirty-two years later than Tiger Woods, so a professional golfer I will never be. But I enjoyed it so much, that I went again, and then again. A year and a half ago I got a membership to a little executive in our neighborhood and recently spent a little more for a more challenging course a little further away. I now own my own clubs and have a handicap (no I won't tell you what it is) and I consider golf a part of my life.

I've gained something out of the game I hadn't expected. My brother-in-law, the husband of sister number two is an avid golfer and somehow, probably with my sister's insistence, we decided to go golfing together. He was always one of those relatives who I thought well of and saw at every family function. But he and I didn't necessarily share any commonalities, so I wouldn't say we had a friendship.

But over the course of many, many rounds of golf over the past three years, that has all changed. As a matter of fact, if there ever were a golf buddy, he would be mine. He has taught me to appreciate the nature of a golf course. He cheers me when I'm doing well and helps me through when I can't make a clean swing all day. We smoke a cigar and go over the latest events of the family, our careers, news, and so much more. We get frustrated at the slowpokes and drunks and try to stay out of the way of the aces. We talk technique, and compare clubs and brag about shots we made when the other wasn't around. If you had told me in high school I was going to become an avid golfer and my brother-in-law was going to be my main man on the course, I would have probably laughed out loud. But that is exactly what happened and he has become one of my most prized friends.

There is no one alive I would rather golf with.

I say no one alive because there is one man who I didn't golf with, one man who got my scorn when he was in the game and I was not, one man who could barely watch the game on television without my heavy sighs of discontent.

My father.

I so regret not playing a few rounds with my dad before he died. All I remember about his game is that he would come back from a day of eighteen, pissed to the end of the world about the course. I wish I could go back and walk the fairways with him, encourage him through his rough spots and cheer him when he nailed a shot.

This year I was able to play the course where he played. Every step, every moment, every stroke felt special because I knew my father had walked the same path, stepped up to the same tees and eyed the same greens.

And every time I play with my brother-in-law I hope Dad's there watching because it feels like a tribute to him.

Once, when he was young, Halsey's father told him a string of stories about golf. They were ridiculous tales and Halsey had a hard time sitting still. He thought of calling his father a liar, because golf was all Halsey ever wanted to do. But his father was so serious that the boy sat quietly and let his father say what he had to say.

"Golf was once a gentleman's game," his father started out one morning when Halsey said he wanted to start his training that summer and attend the academy at the earliest age, twelve, which was four years away. "It was played merely as a sport and did not have the global implications it has today.

"The best historians have estimated the origins of golf to go back approximately seven or eight thousand years, somewhere in the first millennium, although with no records beyond the great wars, no one can be certain."

"What started the great wars, daddy?" Halsey had asked. His father shook his head.

"That also is lost. My best guess is we just got to big. We were so crowded we went a little nuts and just lashed out at each other."

"If we had golf then, that wouldn't have happened," the boy said and he saw a gleam of pride in his father's eyes.

"Yes and it is a noble thing you want to do, Son. Please don't interrupt."

Golf was a gentleman's game at one time. The courses were made of green grass and beautiful trees with lakes beside them. People devoted acres upon acres of beautiful land to these courses, consuming valuable resources to keep them pretty for the golfers. The ball was close to the size it is now, but the hole at the end, and there were many holes, twenty or thirty at least, was the size of my fist.

So the golfers would carry their clubs on their back and walk around the course, no more than ten miles worth, and hit their ball to these holes. It is said they had four-dozen clubs, so these men must have been strong, if not the soldiers we have today.

This strange thing I was told by my grandfather and I'm not sure if he was losing his mind, because it was very late in his life. But he told me once that in golf, balls would be lost and the golfer would simply pull another from his bag of clubs and continue playing. It's almost as if saving the ball was not part of the game. And the players would all take turns, keeping perfectly still when it wasn't their turn, like a statue, and saying kind words to each other.

Halsey began to ask about the hazards and his father put up a hand.

They had none, no true hazards anyway. The courses were perfectly safe. But there is a legend of some sort of giant cat who prowled the courses once, so I suppose that was a danger.

Halsey said he didn't understand why anyone would want to play such a game and his father only nodded in agreement, their imaginations failing to make sense of the ancient golf.

Halsey, then eight years old, sat through the stories, squirming in his chair.

And on this day of his first match, at the age of twenty-three, he thought back on those stories and they seemed even more ridiculous.

He stood, side by side with three other golfers that day, four vying countries. Other than the colors of their uniform, his blue, the United East player in red, the player from Central Strip in pale orange and the Taipei man in white, the players were dressed and equipped exactly the same. He took inventory, checking his club slung securely across his back. A climbing rope hung at his side, fifty meters worth. His shoes were spiked with the regulation two-inch metal prongs that would hold him to a forty-five degree incline almost no matter what the terrain. He had a helmet, although recent legislation called for the removal of the helmets altogether. They apparently thought it took away from the realism of the game if one couldn't get his head bashed. But the camera and microphone sat within the helmet, so until they moved those, Halsey's head was protected. His knees and elbows were padded and strapped to his eyes were the glasses that would allow him to see with scant moonlight. The pills in his zippered vest would sustain him for a week and there were heat strips the size of his thumb, each capable of eight hours of radiant warmth.

To his left and right, stadiums filled with twenty stories of spectators to watch the first mile of the match. They roared as the players walked towards the tee, each detaching their club and approaching the four balls already in place, the color of each matching the color of their uniform and country.

He looked out over the yellow expanse of the course and swallowed. Most of it was wasteland. He knew there would be pockets of radiation to avoid, land mines planted just for the occasion and plenty of poisonous and carnivorous species waiting for their arrival. This course was an endurance course and any of them would be lucky to finish within the week's ration supply.

Three announcers spoke in alternating sentences in three different languages over a sound system that quieted the restless crowd. The first was Halsey's language.

"Ladies and gentlemen," the voice boomed. "Welcome to the sixth match of the year!"

The crowd jumped to their feet simultaneously, screaming and pumping their arms in the air. Halsey noticed the stands were also divided by color, high, cement walls between each, no doubt to keep the fans from destroying each other in their growing frenzy. He could smell the heat and sweat pouring off the mad-eyed spectators, and the headiness of it turned his stomach.

"On this day we begin the match on the treacherous Delaney course, a course famed for it's destruction of the human spirit as well as the human body." The crowd cheered again, the sound of their screams numbing Halsey's ears.

"There will be only one victor in this battle. Our four noble warriors today will vie for their country's right to the new Atlantic Gas Line built by Greenland and for sale today for a hundred and fifty years of use and absolution of all current debt. It was open to all. And these four have come forward to fight. The hole has been placed somewhere between the thirty-eighth and thirty-ninth parallel sixty-four point six miles into the wasteland."

Halsey and the others put the calculations into the watch/compass/radiometer/ball-finder on their wrist. An entire parallel! Halsey was hoping for something more straightforward for his first mission. He thought the guy from Central Strip had the same feelings, as he was young like Halsey. The other two, veterans, displayed no emotion at all. He had also hoped for something nobler than rights to a gas line. But his training pushed the thoughts of doubt from his mind.

Finally, the four balls sat ten feet apart and the four players stood at the ready, their clubs waiting for the signal, the fierce, ear-piercing whistle, to draw back and downswing into the ball, sending it the first seven hundred yards towards their ultimate goal. Halsey was in the number two slot between the veterans. The other rookie stood at number four.

The signal cut through the air and Halsey drew back and put all his strength and a lifetime of training into that swing. His contact was good and his ball went straight and high, arcing out of sight in the right general direction.

He was so enthralled by his shot, Halsey didn't see the attack from the two veterans until it was much too late. Instead of swinging, they used the space of time of the whistle to approach his tee box and use their club to break his ribs and shatter his collarbone. As he lay broken on the ground, utterly defeated, his last view was the Central Strip player sprinting down the hill after his ball and, more importantly, away from the two veterans who had made chase.

His last thoughts were of a green field surrounded by trees and lakes, and four gentlemen walking leisurely after their shots.

CHAPTER NINETEEN – SPEED OF TIME

That could have almost been the beginning of Running Man Part Two, a sequel to Stephen King's Bachman short story and movie The Running Man. By the way, if you ever want to read some extremely disturbing, but fantastically written short stories, get the Bachman Books. There is one in there, The Long Walk, which has stuck in my brain since I was in high school. I wonder how much of my dementedness can be directly attributed to my reading of Stephen King when I was especially vulnerable and my brain neurons weren't quite attached.

Thank you Mr. King!

I have always loved stories about time travel. I loved stretching my mind over the paradox of it all and thinking about what might truly happen if we screwed with our own pasts. Infinite alternate universes are a blast and one great example of this is Kaleidoscope Century by John Barnes. It's twisted and a great ride. But whether a movie, short story, novel or television show, if it has an element of traveling through time, I'm usually good to go.

I've always been acutely aware of the passage of time, tuned in to the seconds passing, the minutes, hours, days and years. I have an impeccable sense of timing when it comes to orchestrating different events, a timing stemming probably from a combination of my dozen years in a radio and my millions of quarters in video games.

I would often complain to my father about the speed of time, wishing it would slow down just a smidge. He just laughed at me. He would tell me, warn me really, that time moved faster and faster the older a person is and that I was in for a shock and I should enjoy time at its current speed.

He was right, of course, as anyone with any age at all will no doubt attest. Time speeds up as we get older. I'm only halfway or less through my little life and it already feels like the years are ticking off like months.

I wish there was some way to slow it down.

I think there is.

I have a theory. Each time I share this theory I get blank stares like I'm trying to attribute suntans to the consumption of macaroni and cheese. But I believe in this and I'm pretty sure it's accurate.

I believe that our concept of time, not the actual passage of time, but how we perceive it, is directly linked to the originality of our current experience. I often use the trip to illustrate this.

Let's say you are going to grandma's new house. She lives two hours away on a road you've never traveled. You've got a list of directions and a vague sense of what her house looks like, maybe color and the kind of car out front. But that's about it. You are embarking on a new journey.

On your way there, the trip seems to drag on and on. By the time you arrive you're tired and it feels as if you've been behind the wheel all day instead of the two hours your watch indicates.

You have your visit. Grandma makes her delicious, homemade cookies and you stay over sleeping under the same afghan you enjoyed as a child.

The next morning you leave, dreading the trip, but ready to get it behind you.

But something happens on the way home. You recognize that grocery store. You remember the town you came through, the one with the two stop signs and the old-time post office on the corner. You recall the bend in the road where the two lanes mercifully turned into four and then back again.

And before you know it, you're home.

See, I believe very strongly that routine speeds up time because the human brain doesn't have to process it. Our gray matter just skips right over it. It's like driving home from work the same way every time. You get home and you can't remember the drive, because your brain was on autopilot. How can we quantify time that we didn't even experience?

So, if you want to slow time down, make sure you break your ruts and routines. Do something new as often as possible. I had an instructor who claimed he never took the same way to work twice. I don't know if that could be done, but he was on the right track and you can bet his life is moving slower than someone who drives the same route every day.

Looks like I'm running out of time in this chapter. Here's a quick story.

When I regained consciousness a rainbow of colors strobed against my eyelids before I even opened them. It was like a madman's dream and I remembered Willy Wonka and the trip on the boat through the infinite cave of liquid chocolate.

"He's awake," a familiar voice said over the noise of the machine buzzing happily under my modified dentist's chair.

I tried to open my eyes and realized I couldn't. My arms and legs wouldn't move either. I was paralyzed, although I didn't know at that moment if it was the drug they fed me before the trip or if I was now a permanent quad.

"Chaim," the voice said. "Calm yourself. You are back and you are going to be fine as long as you don't give yourself a heart attack. Your heart is beating nearly one hundred a ninety-five per minute right now. Calm yourself. This will all be over in a moment."

I tried to calm myself, but since I was completely without physical control I couldn't do anything. So I tried to distract my mind by visualizing the calmest thing I could come up with, which was the feel of my grandpa's rocking chair, padded with two giant flannel pillows, always set in the window to catch the lazy afternoon sun.

"That's it," the voice told me. "Excellent. Whatever you're doing, it's working."

Two hours later I was in a hospital bed in one of the rooms just off the laboratory where time travel had become a reality just one day earlier.

Dr. Levi Wallace, without a doubt the smartest man I have ever met, came into my room shortly after the drug wore off and I regained control of my body. As he walked in with a clipboard under his arm - all six foot six of him, a giant black man with a shiny, bald head and piercing black eyes - he smiled a huge smile and pumped his fist in the air.

"We did it, Chaim," he said. "You are the first man in history to set foot in the future."

"Actually," I said, my voice strange in my ears. "The place was crawling with people. One thing we definitely don't fix five-hundred years from now is the overpopulation of the world."

Levi laughed, uneasily I thought. He had an air of nervousness, of dishonesty in him that I didn't remember before. He was acting like a kid trying to figure out if mom and dad knew what he had done.

"What is it?" I asked. "What's going on?"

"What? Oh, nothing, nada. Nothing at all really. Just that you know how things turned out for me with the experiment. You know how it all turned out and I'm anxious. I want to know what happened. Did you stick to the plan?" He sat down, folding his dramatically long legs in half and popping a pen out of the clipboard to take notes. He was still holding back, but I let it go.

"Yes, I had twenty-four hours as you guessed before I was pulled back. I woke up at night in a city street. It was dark and quiet and not many people were around. Well, not many for the number I saw the next morning. There was certainly a small crowd about, maybe a couple hundred people lining the streets, walking about, you know."

Levi made a motion that he did know and would I please hurry it up.

"Okay, the language was the same, so that was good, but there were lots of different languages. English was still the main one I think. I kept low until the morning and then asked around for a library, which is not what they call it now, by the way. Finally someone got it from my description. It's called a port there. So I go to this port and I'm supposed to plug in, apparently, but obviously I don't have a plug. And we head on to plan B where I start trying to peddle the gold. Then it got weird."

I stopped and took a breath, my voice already feeling worn out from the conversation.

"Okay, I go to this place where on the outside it has written in what must have been fifty languages, Pawn Exchange. Can you believe they still use the word pawn? I go inside and pull out the little hunk of gold you gave me and this guy, or girl I'm not sure, just about loses his lunch all over me. From his reaction I'm going to guess they don't have a lot of available gold in the future, or maybe it has some other use we don't have or something. He says something in another language, maybe French, and then not sixty seconds, I'm telling you, not one minute later two men in purple uniforms come through the front door and grab me."

"Shit," Levi said.

"Yeah no kidding. They tell me, in English thank goodness, to be calm and that they must retain me for further briefing. They're all serious and stuff. In fact, now that I think of it, I don't remember seeing anybody laugh the whole time I was there. Not a very happy place."

"Got it," he said, writing on his clipboard. "Go on. What happened?"

"Well, I'm sorry to say, Doc, but I spent the rest of my time in this little room, being questioned by these guys about where and when I was from. I tried to be evasive at first, but they already knew so much. It was almost like they were waiting for me. And since I didn't have the plug or connector or whatever, I could hardly argue the point. From what I gathered they are all wired from birth. They knew your name, can you believe it?"

If Levi wasn't black, I know his face would have gone white. He looked terrified.

"What did they say," he managed.

"Nothing, but they just brought you up, like I was your employee or something. They seemed to think a lot of you, you know. Like you were important or something. Maybe you are in their history books as the first time traveler."

"You're the first time traveler," he said, almost whispering.

114

"Right. Anyway, they held me there, fed me bland food that looked like cardboard boxes and I drank an odd alcoholic drink that tasted like licorice. I pissed a couple of times in a stand up toilet and then I woke up back here, paralyzed."

"Not much to go on I'm afraid," Levi said both disappointed and relieved I thought.

I then remembered the item.

"Oh crap," I said. "I forgot." I reached into my pocked and pulled out a black marble.

"I pocketed this." I handed it to Levi who took it gingerly. "They left it in the room once and I snagged it. I thought maybe it was some technology or something."

Levi turned it in his hand, peering at it.

"They just left it there?" His eyes shot up in sudden surprise.

"Yeah, on a little table. I don't know how they missed it and I never saw them use it for anything. What do you think it is?"

Before he could answer, the blackness of the marble expanded across Levi's hand, down his sleeve. He looked like he was about to scream but in less than a breath it had enveloped his entire body. He was an ebony statue of himself for a second and then he just, melted, disappeared back down into the marble, which was the only thing left.

I never found out, but I figure ol' Doc Wallace had some pretty underhanded plans for the future and the folks there knew about it. So they sent an assassin back with me to finish him off before he really got rolling. Even the marble disappeared after a couple of minutes. I couldn't prove what happened. But the institute let me go because what else were they going to do?

Now days I'm washing dishes down and Phil's. Pay's for shit, but I couldn't be happier.

So what's your story?

CHAPTER TWENTY – DBAYHAOHOWYS

That last story is an adaptation of a book I wrote last year. The book was horrible, but I liked the idea, so that's what I got out of it. I shouldn't say horrible. Books I will never try to publish are "exercises." That's a euphemism I can swallow.

DBAYHAOHOWYS. Looks like Debay Hah Oh Howies, which doesn't mean anything. It's actually a phrase my father told me several times during my childhood. This would be on the healthy cynicism side of my dual personality. I would be trying to convince him of something I saw on television or talk about a "little known fact" I learned at school and he would throw the phrase at me.

"Don't believe anything you hear and only half of what you see." Let's break that down. Don't believe anything you hear. Anything? Wow, you mean everything I hear I should not believe? That's huge. It's a wonder I have any friends at all. Of course my dad believed everything Johnny Carson ever said, so I know he didn't follow this all the time. And only half of what you see. Well that's probably a higher percentage now than when the saying was originated. Maybe it should be, "Don't believe anything you hear and only ten percent of what you see."

Speaking of origination, I can't find it. I went on the web and searched and searched and all I found out was that there are a lot of kids who attribute that saying to their father. I saw some reference to the military so I suppose my dad could have picked it up there, although I saw many more comments regarding politicians. And I found notes about Will Rogers and Mark Twain as the possible authors, but nothing concrete. Looking it up just made it seem common, so let's pretend I didn't.

But I did take the saying to heart and have repeated it to my kids when the time seemed right. Do they listen? Kids really don't, except maybe on a subconscious level. And if they do, don't expect them to walk up to you and say, "Gee Dad, I really got what you were saying earlier. You've really helped me avoid some terrible pitfalls in my life. Thanks." They learn ninety percent by doing and ten percent by instruction. That's just life and all we can do is hope they survive the rough spots.

Moira was running away from home and that's all there was to it. She'd had enough of her parents' rules and restrictions. All she wanted was a little independence. She was nearly a full-grown woman anyway, so what was the difference? Were they going to hold her down until the last possible moment and then let her flail about the world, unknowing of anything? Today was the day. She'd had enough.

Never mind that she was just ten years old.

She had worked out the details. Mr. Piggy had twenty-six dollars and seventy-two cents, most of which she got for her tenth birthday in June, just two months ago. If she stretched it, she could buy a bus ticket to the next town and cover a couple of meals. But by then she'd be working as a shoe shiner or gas attendant or if she was really lucky, a window washer for one of those really tall buildings. The next town was Bartley and she thought they had big buildings, so that would be best. It had to pay well and she was not afraid of heights.

She packed light, just one change of clothes smashed in her big purse and the money. She also packed extra two extra pair of socks and an extra pair of undies in case she missed the Laundromat for more than a day. She wasn't going to be gross about this.

She decided to walk to the bus station because she didn't want anyone stealing her bike, which she also got for her birthday. If she ever decided to return home, maybe for a visit, she'd like the bike to be there. But that would be in a long, long time. Right now, she just had to get to the station, which would take a while walking.

Midnight. When the clock crossed over midnight and she was sure her parents were asleep, she'd sneak out her bedroom window and start out on her own. By the time she reached the station, the sun would be coming up and she would get her ticket first thing.

After her mother, who was being way too nice, tucked her in bed she got up and dressed and set out everything she would need. At the last minute she decided she'd bring the book she was reading, Nancy Drew and The Case of the Silver Buttons, because she didn't want to be bored. Besides, she wanted to find out what the deal was with those silver buttons.

Just before twelve, she remembered her toothbrush. She had to undress, put on her nightie, pretend she had to go to the bathroom, which it turned out she did, and grab it on her way back. Then she put her travel clothes back on and waited out the last few minutes of her life at home, under the rule of the two adult tyrants in the other room. Boy oh boy were they going to be sad when they didn't find her the next day.

She left no note. She started a couple, but they sounded like she liked them too much and she didn't want them to think they were some great set of parents. They weren't. They never let her do what she wanted to do. Never!

Five past midnight and she realized she was past due for her exit. She checked her items one last time, gave her teddy - who was too big to carry - a big hug and kiss, and slipped out her window.

The air was clean and quiet in the middle of the night. There was a light breeze, but it was still summer, so the breeze felt good on her face and arms. She wondered briefly if she should have packed a jacket for when the cold season hit, but decided she'd be making enough money to buy a new coat or jacket when the time came. She started down the street where she had grown up. It looked different in the dark, the really late quiet dark of just past midnight. The shadows seemed bigger and the houses seemed darker.

"Stop it, Moira," she whispered to herself and set a quick pace towards downtown and the bus station.

Sometimes she would hear a noise and be sure someone was walking behind her. But when she turned and stood still, listening with her heart beating heavily in her chest, she saw nothing at all. And twice, while still in her own neighborhood, a dog spotted her from the backyard of a neighbor's house and barked wildly until she was well down the street.

When she left the subdivision and came to streets that had stop lights, the traffic picked up. She counted between cars going by and sometimes she didn't even make it to ten before another passed. She tried not to eye the cars as she went because she didn't want the drivers to see how young she was, so she kept her head down and tried to walk like an adult would walk, although she had no idea what that was. But no one stopped or even slowed down to check on her so she was able to walk quickly through town.

It didn't take her six hours to reach the bus station so when she got there it was still very dark. She wished she had brought a watch, but she didn't have one. Somewhere in her room was a heart pendant her old boyfriend Jake had given her last year. It had a small clock inside the pendant, but she didn't know where it was. She thought she might have thrown it away when they broke up.

She hid across the street from the station in a little alley between a pawnshop and a tattoo parlor. She watched the late nighters or early morningers come and go into and out of the bus terminal.

Every fifteen minutes or so, Moira wasn't certain, a bus would pull in just as another was pulling out. She had to get on one of those buses and she'd be long gone.

Time went by and the buses came and went, came and went. The sky turned from black and starry to purple to deep blue as the sun got ready to push its way up. Moira had not moved from her spot. She was sleepy now, exhausted from her trip. Though she knew it would hamper her progress, all she could think about was her warm and cozy bed with her teddy snuggled up and her parents sleeping in the other room. She sat on a curb in the alley and leaned against the tattoo shop. She felt her eyes pulling down and realized she was falling asleep. She pinched her own arms to keep her eyes open, which worked at first. But soon she forgot to pinch and in a moment she was asleep.

"Moira," the voice of Moira's mother said. Moira opened her eyes and there was her mom, standing over her. Moira jumped and sat up quickly, looking around, confused. She was in her room, in her bed, still wearing her runaway clothes. "Honey, it's time to get up," her mom continued. "I've got breakfast cooking in the kitchen. Why don't you brush your teeth and come on down. It's pancakes today."

Unable to think of what else to do, Moira got up, brushed her teeth and went to the kitchen, smelling the pancakes long before she saw the giant stack in the middle of the kitchen table.

Her father was there, working on his own plate, chewing thoughtfully and staring out the window into their front yard. When he saw Moira he smiled.

"Rough night?" he asked. Moira nodded slightly.

"I want you to know that we love you very much."

Moira was silent.

"And you should know I followed you to the bus station last night."

Moira's mouth opened, but she couldn't think of anything to say.

"And you're grounded for three months."

Moira's dad went back to his pancakes without another word; her mother humming quietly to herself as she loaded the dishwasher with the previous night's dirties.

The little girl tried not to smile.

CHAPTER TWENTY-ONE – I'M NO SALESMAN

Moira was smiling at the end because all children want rules. They want parents to pay attention to them, to set guidelines, to create consequences. Well, let's be fair, not every kid wants that. I know I didn't. But I'm sure every kid today wants that. Don't they? See, the thing is, they don't know they want it. It's ironic that a child can hate their parents for doing the very thing that keeps kids from going absolutely nuts. And as time goes by and I watch the development of my four, I'm starting to think that deciding how much discipline to give each child (don't kid yourself into thinking they all should be treated equally... unless you're making clones) and when to give it are two of the most important aspects of parenting. Moira needed to have her father follow her, let her stretch her opposition, explore her mutiny and learn more about herself.

And that's all she wanted.

We hope.

Nobody knows for sure.

My father was one of those men with sales in their blood. He was absolutely born to sell, infused with all the proper DNA to pitch and close, programmed with the armor to accept rejection gracefully and given the gift of gab and the bigger gift of paying attention.

I only witnessed this in his latter years because he was forty-five when I was born. For most of my growin'-up-years the man sold on the road, traveling up and down I-5. He sold adverts for the maps at gas stations and then he managed a group of men who sold them.

I think twice he took sister number four and I with him to

Sacramento to stay in the hotel - I always thought of it as Dad's Hotel - and swim in the pool and play in the elevator till they kicked us off. I loved the candy machine and telling the waitress to give my compliments to the chef. I was about ten when we took that last trip. I remember because my sister was trying to convince some boys in the pool she was fourteen when she was, as I pointed out at the top of my lungs, only twelve.

My dad began managing his sales guys from home when I was twelve or thirteen. I heard strange, exotic names like Artois and Dunnigan on my dad's end of phone conversations and imagined them to be strange, exotic places. They're not.

I didn't know it at the time, but listening to him yell at those poor men over the phone for those four or five years had an effect on me that wouldn't manifest itself until I was well into my thirties.

Despite the fact that my dad's superior salesmanship supported my vast, uncountable family and me for decades, I had no respect for the job. Isn't that awful? I would exclaim over and over that I could never do sales. I couldn't handle the rejection. I wasn't that type. That type, in my brain, was the polyester-wearing, plastic-grinning, hair-combing monkey constantly stereotyped in movies and television. Even though my sweet father had none of those qualities, that's how I pictured a salesman.

So, fast-forward to me with four children of my own and the realization that working at a radio station was both not going to go anywhere and would never make enough money to support this giant family for which I had voluntarily opted. How did that happen?

I quit my job just after my fourth was born and started looking for another line of work. And yes, that was a really stupid thing to do considering the previous paragraph.

Three months later, not a job in sight, not even on the distant horizon, I got desperate. I called my previous employer and asked for my old job back. Of course it had been filled.

Three months and two weeks later, I got phenomenally desperate. I was actually thinking of Micky D's or BK or anything else that would bring in money. Our savings had disappeared and if I didn't find a job almost immediately, we were going down like a rocket ship out of fuel.

I got that job, the next day, from the bank where I now work. I got a sales job. It was probably the only situation hopeless enough that could have forced me to accept a job in sales. Otherwise, I would have never broken the shell around my dormant skills, skills I learned while I was not listening to my father coach his trodden salesmen.

And those talents have nothing to do with polyester clothes or a permanent smile.

Those first few weeks at the bank, it was as if my father was in my ear, talking to me, coaching me as I spread my mildew-covered wings and tried the impossible.

"When you first go in to a business, find something unique about it. Point it out to the prospect and take a genuine interest in their operation. Learn something."

"Be friendly and optimistic and know when to shut your damn mouth. The salesman who shoves his product down a customer's throat is a Neanderthal."

"Your relationship with your prospect is more important than you or your product. And you can't fake it. So you better like people. They will eventually be the source of nearly all your new sales."

"Believe in what you are selling. If you don't, go sell something else. And never try to sell your product to someone who doesn't need it."

I entered my job and broke records, and then broke my own records. I bet my boss one night over dinner that I could hit five million in loans in one quarter and he offered my wife and me a week in Hawaii if I succeeded. The previous record was about three million. That was June of 2004. The week in Maui in October of that year was wonderful.

Three months later, the bank promoted me to a full commercial lender with a thirty million dollar portfolio of my own.

And I thought I couldn't sell.

Thanks Dad.

Misty's last day of life was nothing like what she had planned.

Even in the twenty-second century, there was no accounting for planning and no way to anticipate every single possibility. But Misty was smart, much smarter than most, and she thought she could guarantee herself a great last day.

She planned for weeks, working out the five aspects of any event: who, what, where, when and why. She gave careful consideration to every detail and even worked up contingency plans for different anomalies. Before she was done, she had a small tomb of data, schedules, lists and diagrams all cross-referenced for easy access with a complete index in the back.

She never got past page one.

It was still dark outside when the terrorists took over her building. They announced on the COM that the building was being held and that no one would be leaving until their demands were met. They didn't explain what those were, but Misty imagined money, transportation and some sort of immunity or other. They did say they had explosives enough to level the building and all one hundred and fifty residents if the sun set and they had not been satisfied.

"This is not going to be my last day," Misty said to her cat, which looked up at her through Calico fur and meowed tentatively.

Misty dressed and tried her door, which had been given a new security code and remained shut. Her window opened, but she was on the sixth floor. She looked over the ledge, a small, stone patio suspended in mid-air, identical to the ones below it and the one above it. Three men in black uniforms stood at the ground level. They had guns.

"Okay, no going that way," she whispered.

She went back into her apartment in time to hear the terrorist announce that they were going to search the building, room by room and that anyone showing any resistance would be shot and hung from their own ledge as a warning.

"Crap."

Misty thought of the roof and the distance to the building next to hers.

"Maybe."

She found her broom and knocked against her ceiling. She counted ten raps and then went outside and looked up. Nothing.

She went back in and tried another ten knocks. Then another ten just for good measure before she checked again.

"Hello," she whispered.

"Stop doing that," a voice came back, the voice of Mr. Johan, whispering angrily. "You're going to get us killed."

"Hell with that. Today is my last day. And it's not going to be by the hand of these bums. Lower a rope down or something. I'm going up to the roof."

"No way."

"Do it or I will make so much noise up here they will have no choice but to open fire on both of us."

Misty waited. After a few minutes a knotted sheet came down the side of the balcony above hers. She grabbed it, tested its strength and quickly scrambled up and into Mr. Johan's apartment.

She heard the rattle and cock of guns and turned around to see three of the terrorists standing in his apartment, guns trained on her, Mr. Johan sitting meekly at his pale blue kitchen table, wearing nothing but a long tee-shirt and white, fluffy slippers.

"Pussy," she said to him.

"It wasn't his fault, Lady," one of the terrorists said. Their mouths were covered so she wasn't immediately sure which. "We were covering the top floor first. Now you've got two choices."

"Is one of them to get the hell out of here?"

"You can either go back to your room or we can throw you over the ledge."

Misty steeled herself against her fear.

"Listen, guys, today is my last day. You think I want to spend my last day here, in this damn building, worrying about when you're going to blow us all up? I couldn't care less. I'm gone anyway. You might as well throw me. At least I'll get a thrill on the way down."

The terrorists were looking at each other. Misty didn't understand. Finally the leader, the speaker faced her again.

"This is your last day?"

"Yup, or what's left of it anyway, thanks for nothing. I should be skinny dipping in the capitol fountain by now, tossing my tits at every guy I see. You know I have a whole book of things I'm supposed to do today? Every minute counts."

"Come with us," he said and they grabbed her and forced her at gunpoint back down into her apartment.

When they reached her room they threw a small black bundle at her. She unwrapped it and held it out. It was one of their uniforms.

"And you want me to, what with this?"

"Put it on."

"Why?"

"Do you know why we're here?"

"To ruin what's left of my life?"

The leader took off his hood and face-wrap. He was a beautiful man, dark hair and eyes, olive skin, a slight shadow of new-beard across his face.

"We're protesting population control. We're here to prolong your life."

"So you're going to kill people?"

He laughed.

"No. It's a ruse, for publicity sake. We've got an escape route in the subsystem below the city all set up. We're searching the building for short-timers to offer them a place in our organization."

"Cute."

"We've all gone past our last day."

"You have?"

"Yes. How would you like to take the next few years to do what's in your last day book."

Misty had never considered living past twenty-nine and three-hundred-and-sixty-four days. She was suddenly extremely excited, or possibly turned on by her captor. She wasn't entirely sure which.

"Keep talking," she said.

CHAPTER TWENTY-TWO – PROVIDE

Who knows where we will be as a society and as a world in a few hundred years? The answer is nobody. There are events that will occur between now and, say, 2305 that we cannot conceive. So it's a pleasure to traipse about in the imagined future and see what becomes.

A father should provide for his family. As old fashioned as that may sound, I still believe it. When my beautiful wife becomes a wildly successful screenwriter and I don't have to do much more than sit on my duff play with the kids in our own personal arcade, I will still feel the need to provide for my family. It's part of who I am and certainly was also part of my father's makeup as evidenced by his work schedule. To provide for his family, my father drove every Monday the three and a half hours to Sacramento, coming home every Friday, living in a hotel during the week. That's some kick-ass providing.

And I know we had ups and downs financially when I was growing up, but I couldn't tell you when those times were. My dad never gave that stuff away. Which also meant he wasn't the best money manager and wasn't opposed to running up a pile of debt if the need arose... or the want. I am also terrible with money. I'm lucky I found a thrifty wife (euphemism) who is not prone to impulse buys and is willing to balance the checkbook and pay the bills. Because if it was left to me, we'd be living in our car by now.

But I work hard, and I'm proud that my kids have clothes to wear and food to eat and a real home with a lawn and garage and real live rain gutters that I have to clean but never do.

It's the sixth day of snowfall, and the chimney and attic window are the only parts of the house not buried, and I understand now that this is no ordinary storm and we are probably not getting out alive. I have to decide whether we were going to die in our home or meet our end while making our way down the mountain.

Four years. Four years we have lived in this cabin, isolated from "civilization" just enough to feel alone in the world, but not far enough that we can't purchase our needs, take care of our banking, wire far-off family and get medical treatment six or seven times a year. The winter weather has been difficult at times, prone to high winds and torrential rain. But the snow rarely comes and never sticks more than a day or two. Until one week ago when the stranger came through.

I want to be clear that I am a trusting man. I made the decision early in life to expect the best from people and hell-be-damned whatever happens, happens. Most of the time, I am not disappointed, because most people are good. After Maye and I had Jeremy and then Marianne the next year I must say that some of the trust went out of me. And by the time we moved to the cabin I was ready for a break from my optimism.

When I heard the meek rap on our front door early one evening during a brewing rainstorm my heart felt heavy. And when I opened the great, wooden door on its massive, iron hinges and I saw him for the first time. The clouds seemed darker and the rain heavier and, though I am not a man of psychic experience, I would say I had a foreboding.

Not that he was a menacing fellow. As a matter of fact, he appeared harmless, so much so, that Maye invited him in straightaway to get out of the coming weather. And he was injured.

This man, not five foot five by my reckoning, stood draped in a dirty, white robe that hung down far below his feet, dragging on the ground where it turned almost black from the abuse. His face was pale, some might say translucent, and heavily wrinkled, two small white-blue eyes peering over a white beard combed perfectly straight and traveling down to the middle of his chest. His tiny, pale, wrinkled hands poked out from the robe, one holding a small, hardwood branch he used to steady himself and the other grasping at his chest where a circle of bright red was increasing as I stood there, gawking.

He tried to speak but could not and Maye brought him inside, giving me a look with her giant, gray eyes that said, help or get out of the way. At first, I could only stand.

Once inside, the old man collapsed completely and we could not revive him for two days.

We put him in Jeremy's bed and the children slept with us so he might have his own room. Since Jeremy is only just seven, the bed seemed a bit small, but he fit well enough and there was nothing to be done about it.

Maye and I worked on his chest the best we could. He had been shot, clean through, in the back by some small caliber gun. The back seemed okay and closed up with only two stitches. But the front, where the bullet came out, was a mess. And his skin seemed paper-thin. As I sewed him up that first night, afraid he might die under my hand, I tried to be as dainty as any man could be. I lost track of the stitches, many inside and many out, and when I was done I collapsed next to him in Marianne's bed.

When I woke the next morning, the snowstorm had begun. The flakes were big and thick, so much so the children caught them on their tongue as they fell out of the sky. They built five snowmen lickety split from the foot of new snow on the ground, the likeness of us and the old man. Jeremy begged and begged to go find a hill they might sled, but I said no for which I'm glad. By that afternoon the foot of snow had risen to waist-high on me and up to Jeremy's chest.

We were pretty well snowed in by that night, and on the second night, when the old man finally woke, I could no longer open the door to the outside, nor would I want to. But we had firewood inside for several days, even a week, and the snow had somewhat insulated our little cabin, making it warm like an igloo, so I did not panic.

We had all retired to the main room for dinner when I heard his voice, an almost female voice, like a grandmother might sound, from the other room.

"Hello?" he called. "Hellooooo."

We all jumped up together to see the strange old man. He was sitting in the bed, holding the blanket Maye had given him up to his neck, looking modest and meek. And again, I felt a dark strength within him.

"Helloooo," he said again, looking at us and smiling through a perfect set of snow-white teeth. "You be the saviors of this old heart?" He tapped his mangled chest, the black stitches criss-crossing half-hazard like a child had drawn them there.

"Aye, that is me," I said. "Not pretty, but I think I got all the pieces back in place." I smiled though I didn't feel like smiling. Maye smiled as well, pinning her long, brown hair behind her in a makeshift bun and going fearlessly to his side. She poured him a cup of water and handed it to his shaking fingers.

"Please, have a drink," she said. He took it gratefully and took the whole of it in one draught. She refilled it and he finished that as well.

"Your kindness is boundless and foundless," he said with a chuckle. "I don't know how to thank ye."

And so the niceties went and when he felt well enough the next morning he joined us in the main room for breakfast dressed in clothes of mine which looked like a sack on his frame. I asked him, because my own vulgar curiosity could not contain itself and because he had not offered any information himself, how he came to be bleeding from a gunshot on our front porch. He eyed me with my direct question, his stare palpable on the skin of my face, thick and dark. But then he smiled kindly and laughed.

"There are hunters in this wood," he said. "They are careless with their aim. I was making my way through the thickest forest, hoping to reach a clearing where I might find my bearings. I imagine the man was far away because I didn't hear the explosion of the gun until the damage was well done and over. I tried to cry for his aid but he did not hear me, or did not care to admit he had shot an old man."

"Probably the Smithies down the ridge," Maye said. "They get hungry early in the winter and don't take much time to measure what they've got in their sights."

I nodded, but the old man hadn't answered the part of the question I most wanted to know.

"Why were you here?" I asked.

Again he looked at me. This time the cloud on his face was unmistakable, even Maye seemed to shiver from it.

"I was here," he began, the smile gone from his face. "Because I lost my way. I come through here every year, but never this far south. I got misplaced, maybe in my age, and once I was on this side of the mountain, there was no getting back. I had to come through. I am sorry."

"Why are you sorry," I asked.

"You need to leave me here," he said. "Get off the mountain now before it's too late. But don't take me with you. I must stay here."

"You want us to leave our home to you and scuttle off the mountain?" I asked.

"We've only just settled here," Maye said.

"You did me a kindness and I am trying to return the gift. If you do as I say you will escape the wrath of the storm. If you do not, I will not be responsible for your demise. I can tell you no more."

With that he left us, stunned, to our breakfast and returned to Jeremy's bed.

A fever took him that afternoon and he did not recover. He lays there, in Jeremy's bed, sweating and then shaking as the snow builds higher and higher outside. Soon, an escape from the house will be impossible.

Maye and I have decided to leave the home. We are going to leave him here because we cannot carry him out, small as he is, and we would all surely die with his burden. So we have brought the fire to a crisp blaze and made him as comfortable as possible. Marianne is crying, but I care more of their lives than this stranger and cannot abide her tender heart.

Once out on the roof we see nothing but white. The snow falls so heavily my feet are nearly invisible. I take the hand of my trusting wife and she has tied a rope to each of our children and we leave the chimney and the cabin roof's slight peak, and head in the direction that should lead us down the mountain.

One hundred yards from our home the storm ends. I don't mean it stops. It ends, like a wall has been placed to keep it at bay. The snow has piled up to a great mountain, but I can see bare dirt just a few feet ahead. We all run down the hill and hit the ground. I look up and see blue sky between gray and white clouds. And looking down the mountain I can see almost all the way to the small town where we buy our supplies.

When I turn around I see the white, menacing storm over our cabin, burying it. I don't understand, but I am too happy to pause. We rush down the slope and I feel the darkness of the old man fade behind me.

That happened over a year ago. When the old man died the storm disappeared. And now, it is nearly a new year and the rains won't drop, the cold snap hasn't hit and no snow falls from the sky. People in the town say it's an unusual winter.

But I know the truth.

One of the Smithies shot Old Man Winter last November and the snow is not coming back.

CHAPTER TWENTY-THREE – GET ALONG

I remember one day, my father had listened to sister number four and me battle for the better part of the morning and into the afternoon. When we fought, there was biting and scratching and punching and oodles and oodles of yelling and screaming and crying. Dad got the whole brunt of it. It must have been a Saturday. He was fresh back from Sacramento, exhausted from the week, trying to relax and maybe watch a little tube. And we are spinning through the house like two Tasmanian Devils bent on destroying each other.

He cracked.

I just remember his massive frame descending on us, looming over us as we sat, mid-pinch, on the couch; our mouths both open in an interrupted scream. His face was as red as rare meat and he was shaking with rage.

"Why can't you two just get along?" he screamed.

Believe it or not I almost laughed at him. He was furious, no doubt about it. And this same man had literally thrown me down a long hallway and into my room one afternoon when I refused to clean it. So I knew he was capable of many things. And until he opened his mouth I thought we were in for it.

But the desperation in his plea for us to stop fighting was comical.

As I have found time and again, the things I tortured my father with have come back to torture me as a parent. Knowing that then probably wouldn't have stopped me, but it might have slowed me down a bit.

When our two oldest children were five and six, my daughter and stepson new siblings to each other, part of a brand new family, they fought fiercely. They were both only children up to that point. Daddy's little girl and Mommy's little boy, both used to having whatever they wanted, whenever they wanted it. It's easy to imagine the clashing of those two spoiled personalities.

We had some growing pains.

And there was a particular afternoon, I'm going to say it was a Saturday, when they were biting and clawing and pinching and screaming, when I cracked.

I heard the words coming out of my mouth almost before I could control them.

"Why can't you two just get along!" I screamed it at the top of my lungs. I must have scared the hell out of our apartment neighbor, an older, sweet-as-pie woman who lived alone.

And kick me in the head if they didn't smile when they saw my desperation.

Is there a lesson here?

Yes.

Never let them see you sweat. As soon as they do, and yes I'm talking about your kids, you are dust.

I remember when they all wanted me.

I'm not being a conceited bitch either. They all did want me. And by all, I mean every able-bodied man with half a libido who put their eyes on my bod.

Once, at a concert, I had flirted my way to the front lines. I stood at the edge of the stage, moving my hotness to the heavy rock beat, dancing in my own little space. I noticed as the men around me lost interest in the show to watch me instead. And then, the band stopped.

I'm not kidding. Why, in my current state, would I lie about this? What possible gain would there be save for the pathetic push for a person like me to gain a few seconds of recognition from the likes of you? This is the absolute truth.

For eight years, I had the men of this world by the balls, literally. I flew from continent to continent, traveling about as if I had the key to all the cities in all the countries. I had the key all right. It was this body, or rather what this body was up until three and a half years ago. I had affairs with married movie stars and politicians. I caused some commotion when the tabloid photographers caught a prime minister (I won't say who) with me in the back of his limousine. I was completely naked. The pictures netted the taker almost a million dollars and the issue with my body in it ranked in their top ten of circulation. I didn't see any of it, but I didn't care. I had everything I could ever want.

I ate at the finest restaurants, always for free. I stayed on exotic white sand beaches in the penthouses of the finest hotels. I wore diamond necklaces, rings, earrings, bracelets and broaches, all gifts from my lovers. More dukes and kings gave me open invitations to visit their castle or palace than I can even count. The women hated me but the men didn't care.

I don't know how many marriages I destroyed.

It was a lot.

And I think that is why things have turned out as they have. I now believe in Karma. I also believe I didn't take care of mine.

I never cared who I hurt. Well, almost never.

There was one man, a Spaniard, not particularly beautiful. He had an interesting face, long and narrow with big lips and very bright, dark eyes. His hair went everywhere and I longed to grab it and see what it might feel like to kiss that oversized mouth. He sat a table over from my current man and me as we had lunch at an outside cafe in his native country.

Seducing him took an afternoon, which had never happened. It was because he wouldn't look at me. He must have caught my beauty from the corner of his eye and looked away before he could be overcome. I spoke to him and flirted with him, but he never looked up from his drink or the newspaper he was reading. It was a cool autumn day and he was sweating from the strain of ignoring me. But he did it and I thought I might have lost him. I had to be bold.

When he was finished at the cafe, I sent my current lover on his merry way with a promise for a late night tryst and followed my new interest.

As I had hoped, he went through the city park on his way to wherever he was headed. I skirted in front of him, raced ahead and waited in a partially secluded area with lots of trees and bushes on either side of the otherwise empty path. By the time he caught up, I wore nothing but a pink lace bra and matching g-string panties. I flipped my hair as his eyes rested on mine and then trailed down my body. I had him.

We made love all that afternoon, right there in the park. It was some of the most amazing I have ever experienced. We met again and again over the next couple of weeks. I knew he was married, though he didn't speak once of his wife.

Then one evening, after an intense couple of rounds in my hotel room, he and I were lazing on the balcony, which sat one floor above the street. He was smoking a sweet-smelling cigar and we were both wrapped in the white terry cloth robes.

I heard a woman from below call his name.

I looked down and there she was, also a beautiful woman, though plain. The pain in his wife's eyes shot up off the street and poured over our perfect night together. I started to smile, as I have never felt bad about ruining an unfaithful man's marriage. But then another voice called up.

"Daddy?" a little girl's voice said. I looked and next to the grief-stricken woman was a girl, maybe eight or nine. Big, strange, tears coursed down her cheeks, confusion twisting her eyes and mouth.

I didn't care about the woman. But I had a daddy once and for a moment that little girl's pain was my pain. For a moment I understood what I was doing and why.

The moment was gone, soon enough, and I mostly forgot about the little girl.

Today, with what has happened, I think about her a lot.

See, I was back in the states three and a half years ago when I met up with a quiet, tough, motorcycle-riding guy who stunk like a dead dog. Like the rest, he was overwhelmed by me and the next thing I knew I was behind him on his bike going to some place called Sturgis for a big get together. Despite his smell (remember I had spent a good amount of time in France) I liked him in his black leather and silver-tipped cowboy boots.

I was enjoying myself, really getting off on the noise of the bike and the wind and the outside smells whipping by us.

The bike went down on a high desert road when a truck driver fell asleep halfway through his night and forgot to pull over first. Dead dog turned to avoid him, thinking a little road rash would be better than a head-on.

We tumbled.

I woke up in a hospital with several broken bones. I couldn't move for days. I had bandages all over my body and was told there was a fire when the bike exploded. I was lucky to be alive, they told me. Over and over, again and again, they said I was lucky to be alive, that it was a miracle that I survived at all. After two or three days I realized most of my face had been wrapped in the same white gauze I was seeing on my arms and legs.

After a week, real pain set in where my skin had been sufficiently burnt. I don't know why it took so long. Maybe shock, maybe they were giving me more medication in the beginning. I couldn't say.

What I can tell you is the pain was overwhelming.

I spent two years in that hospital. I was completely alone.

They would have thrown me out long before that, but I still had my diamonds and I cashed those in for medical treatment.

When I did finally get out, I had nothing. My small cache of wealth was depleted to about five hundred dollars. I had no transportation. I had no friends. I had no family. I had no lover (Dead dog died in the accident.) What I did have, for the first time in my life, were scars. Half my face had been washed away on the cold, desert asphalt. Most of my right side, as a matter of fact, looked like someone did a poor job of erasing it with a dirty eraser.

I looked, smeared.

And I still do. Eighteen months later, people avoid me when they see me. Children are afraid of me, adults' noses twitch or their mouths curl in disgust or, worse, pity.

"What do you want," the little girl asked. I knew she was swayed, somewhat by my story. But I also knew her pain and loss ran deeper than mine.

"I just want you to know I'm sorry I did that to your daddy. And I want you to know he had no chance or choice. I want you to know he was the strongest of all the men I have ever seduced and that you shouldn't blame him for anything."

"I don't."

"Good," I said quickly, hoping for it to be done.

She looked hard at me and then reached up and traced her fingers roughly across my scarred cheek.

"Good for who?" she asked. "Not you. Not me. Not my mother or my father. Especially not him. He died six months ago, you know. Shot his own head off. Because of you. Because of how he hurt my mum and me." She slapped my face with so much force I almost fell. "Go to hell."

The sixteen-year-old girl walked quickly down the cobbled street, back to her school where I had fetched her.

I'd kill myself today, but I think this is my sentence, and I'm committed to taking my punishment in full.

CHAPTER TWENTY-FOUR – MORRIS POND

Every kid should have his or her own Morris Pond.

A Morris Pond is a place that time cannot touch, a place whose smells, sounds and textures are clear in a child's mind, and don't weaken when the child is grown.

A Morris Pond is magical, with hidden secret corners and shadows full of possibilities.

At Morris Pond, imagination is boundless and free.

My first trip to Morris Pond was with my father, at about six years old. I don't think we even had fishing poles. I used the memory of that day for the dream in Chapter 13. What I didn't talk about previously was the absolute quiet.

Morris Pond sits in the middle of a forest of young, straight pines, on the edge of a mountain town. Black Ranch Road leads to the tiny body of water. The road runs long and straight with absurd dips my sweet daddy liked to take at absurd speeds to make his children squeal as his El Dorado's front wheels briefly left the ground. The road is home to nearly all the town's ghost stories, all of which I believed, stories that gave me my first chills.

The brief walk through the trees - their low branches hanging heavy with wet moss - is whisper quiet. Unheard is each step on the ash-colored, damp, packed clay earth. The birds hold their chatter, there is no hint of breeze and as the pond draws closer, even the toads hold their tongue. The only sound is the vague hum of the insects waiting to be swallowed by the scores of dragonflies and trout waiting just below the murky water.

When nature is quiet, when even the animals seem to pay respect to a place, when nature seems to pray to itself, the timelessness becomes part of the guest. I probably visited the pond a dozen times in my young life, maybe less. But I could have gone only that one, first outing with my dad. Because I took part of the soul of the place away with me.

My father may not have realized the gift he gave me, but I'm pretty sure he did. (See Chapter 10)

I regret being too young or too busy or too stupid to give my older children their own magic place because every kid should have their own Morris Pond. I hope they found theirs without me.

From above, the city was beautiful, great spires, towers reaching for the clouds, competing over centuries to be the tallest. The sun glistened off the cities brightest buildings, their mirrored sides tossing the light back and forth, down, down onto the city streets. The streets looked like a crawling mass of vermin from the highest heights, choked with walkers and runners and bikes and cars, all moving with purpose to their destination with no patience for their fellow citizens.

From above it grew, blossomed like a flower, where there was once nothing but prairie wind and wheat stalks. The mass of humanity became its own world, too many millions to count, too many heartbeats to hear. And still they came, drawn to the city by its promise of wealth and opportunity. The city moved day and night, never slowing, never becoming any less active, the sun's thousands of reflections replaced by a hundred million lights that turned the sky to dawn and blew out the stars as if they were a galaxy of timid candles.

One of the buildings, an older building but still magnificent, is topped with a playground, which is surrounded by a giant cyclone fence. The playground is painted green, but no grass grows there. All the best and safest pieces of kid pleasure sit waiting for the screaming, squealing mass of underdeveloped humanity to descend on them twice a day, nearly every day. The monkey bars and rings and slides and ladders. The giant tires and swings and teeters and boxes of synthetic sand. A hundred children could play on the top of this middle-of-the-road building and there would be room for a hundred more.

The school occupies the top three floors of the building and children who go there often receive elementary, high school, undergraduate and graduate level education without ever leaving them.

Next come the residences, the families of the children above, placed in spacious if not completely similar homes big enough to hold three generations or more. Nearly half of the building is consumed by a simple place to leave. Extensive camera networks keep the occupants in line if the sense of community should sometimes fail them.

Traveling down the throat of the building, the great central elevator network, the homes evolve into offices, first the largest, richest companies with the most important, most influential people in the building, if not the city. This being such a mediocre building, chances are rare that a political potentate or citywide CEO would bother working here. The offices become smaller and more practical the closer the levels get to the city street.

Below the offices, stores of every type materialize; anything from groceries to clothing to the latest computer creation can be bought without ever leaving the building.

Restaurants and entertainment are just above the ground level so non-residents can enjoy them without getting too far off the ground. This particular building has almost four-dozen restaurants counting the fast food stands and pizza joints. Most buildings have more, but this building is one of those built many years ago and well beyond its prime. The entertainment includes nightclubs, dive bars, theaters, stages, symphonies and virtual sports of a hundred different varieties.

At ground level is security where humanity comes and goes, often pouring out of the building like a silo dropping grain.

All is at it appears in the building, a finely tuned, purring machine designed to expedite life, make it the most efficient existence possible.

But below the building, under the streets, where the old city once thrived, are the forgotten segments of the civilization, the thorns of blossoming humanity. Dark, quiet halls lit by single, dangling bulbs mark the paths to and from the under-city, stairways rather than elevators travel deeper and deeper underground to more dark halls with dingy walls and scuffed floors and rows and rows of similar, gray doors.

On one of the lowest levels, nearly to the original ground level of the city when it was still just dirt and an idea, one of the thousands of doors opens to a room lousy with sound. The chitter and chatter of machines spills into the hall. An oddly high ceiling in a surprisingly spacious room boasts a handful of bulbs similar to those in the hall. The resulting light is little more than a candle's worth because of the size of the room, but it doesn't slow the machines. The room is cool, insulated by ten million people and ten thousand buildings, but the air is thick with the smell of burning, electric capacitors and the formaldehyde used to preserve the nine dozen bolts of fabric that chaotically decorate the farthest wall.

Sitting at one hundred sewing machines are ninety-one girls and eight little boys, one of the machines down for repair. They sew garments at impossible speeds, each of the children given a specific task for the day; attach this bodice to this skirt, hem these pant legs and attach the belt loops, surge this underlining for tomorrow's assembly. No child is over the age of ten. Ten is the age of freedom. Ten is the age when their parents' debt is paid. Ten is the age when they return to the aboveground life. Besides, after ten years old, their hands are too large for many of the sewing tasks in which this factory specializes. Until then they work every day in this room, eating and sleeping in the barracks next door. The string-thick bands around their necks keep them in line when needed. But they rarely are. They are good workers and the supervisors remind them constantly that the fates of their families rely solely on them.

So they work.

In one of the darkest corners of the factory, one girl, just six years old, works in near darkness. Her fellow workers call her Mouse and the supervisors think it's because she is so small. But they have given her that name because she disappears every night and since she doesn't ever speak, no one knows where she goes. The older kids have tried to stay up, to watch her escape. She simply waits quietly until they doze. If one has the will to watch her the entire night, they are so miserable the next day they never try again. If she were a boy, they might beat her until she showed them. But she's tiny and beautiful, so they let her be.

The truth is she has found a vent in the barracks. It's on the floor and partially covered by her cot. The other children have seen it, but don't expect that is her escape because it looks too small for a person to get through. Indeed it is difficult for Mouse. She has to squirm and wiggle and hold her breath as she drops down into the dark, square, hole. But she makes it through and the vent immediately opens into a corridor that leads into an old air conditioning system, which leads to a room that holds a forgotten freight elevator that travels not just to the surface, but all the way up the spine of the building, behind the elevators everyone else uses.

Each night she takes that elevator to the very top of the building, past the restaurants and stores, beyond the offices and above the grand offices of the important businessmen and women, up through the residences where sometimes she hears laughter through the walls of the elevator shaft and can't help but cry a little, past the college, high school and elementary school and all the way up to the playground with the green painted asphalt and every piece of equipment imaginable.

She doesn't play with any of it. She climbs the highest ladder and lays down on the soft, plastic landing, her little arms supporting her little head as she gazes into the well-lit sky.

She breathes the air and feels the breeze on her face and bare feet.

But mostly she enjoys the quiet. She is surrounded by giant, silent toys, toys which were probably brought up here by the same freight elevator she uses, all of them completely silent, and imagines they are watching over her, keeping her safe from all harm and giving her the strength to work through the next day.

She knows these nights are becoming precious few as she slowly outgrows her hole in the floor. Soon, she will be truly confined to the barracks and the factory, stuck until she turns ten and can rejoin her family.

Until then, she tries to soak up every breath of her own magic place.

CHAPTER TWENTY-FIVE – PROFANITY
(Warning: This chapter contains explicit language.)

My father was a beautiful cusser. I'm fairly certain an entire day did not go by when I didn't hear "God Damn It" (pronounced Gawdaammaatt) several Christs (pronounced kee-rhist) and the occasional Shit. On very rare occasions, when my father was truly mad, had reached a point of exasperation or rage, Fuck would come out. That didn't happen very often and I can't help but think that one of his wives convinced him to keep that one to himself. But once in a while it would slip. That's when I knew I was in serious trouble. As they say in the movie Christmas Story, it was the granddaddy of all cuss words, the F, dash, dash, dash word.

So, probably thanks to my dear ol' dad, I love to cuss. I love spinning profanities, figuring out new ways of saying bad words. I love the self-expression involved with a good string of bad. I like to be vulgar. Most especially and most importantly, however, I love the release of a good cuss word.

If I smash my finger with a hammer and I can't say, for instance, "Fuck, fuck, fuckity fuck," then I'm just lost. If I can't tell a fellow driver, "Kiss my white ass you near-sighted, blue-haired, ugly, motherfucker," I might succumb to real road rage. There are cocksuckers and ass-wipes who need to be recognized in this world. There are shit-heads and prick-heads and dick-heads who might not even be aware of their status. I think fuck is probably my favorite cuss word. It spins out of my mouth like a top and can mean anything from anger to pain to amazement to sex. It's an adjective, a noun and an adverb. Sure, it's an expletive as well, but that is such a narrow view of the grand four-letter word that is F-U-C-K.

I had a college professor, an incredible man named Dalrymple who told great stories. One of those stories was an illustration of why he so hated that word. He traveled back through literary time and explored its root. As the class traveled back with him, we realized the meaning had changed significantly over the years. Apparently the word fuck comes from a root word that used to mean rape. I don't remember his whole story and have failed to find it on Internet searches. Can you imagine typing the word fuck into an Internet search? The meaning of the word is not easy to find among ten billion matches. Besides, all those other sites are distracting, enough to make the searcher forget the reason for the search in the first place.

At any rate, I respected Dalrymple and even considered giving the word up for its previous meaning. But it doesn't mean that to me and taking it out of my vernacular now would be like cutting off my dick, or prick, uh cock, head, one-eyed worm, snake... penis. It's just not going to happen.

My best cussing story happened about eleven years ago when I was with my wife-to-be and future in-laws at Great America in California. The Top Gun was a new ride and I couldn't wait to get on it.

I'm walking through the parking lot, my future mother-in-law next to me, and even from outside the park, we can see the intensity of the Top Gun as it rises and falls, flips and corkscrews, its passengers hanging with feet dangling in mid-air, screaming in fear and fun.

"Mother fuck!" I say in awe. The only person who heard me was the mother of my future wife. How proud was I?

But for the most part I'm able to control my tendency toward vulgarity. I use it when I can and keep it to myself when I need to.

But like my father, I can't say my children have never heard their dad throw down the dark oaths.

The old man sat at his desk, a great, walnut monster big enough to sleep three comfortably. He hunched over the desk, a slight shadow darkening the dark wood from the lamplight in the corner of the small library. Scant warmth brushed against his cheek from the fire burning meekly in the massive hearth. Under his aging eyes were three parchments: a will and testament, an official decree and a love letter.

He sighed heavily, his lungs laboring, rasping against the effort, his gray hairs, long and unkempt as if he just rose from a dream-filled sleep, moved like tiny fingers grabbing at his rancid breath.

"What do I do Marie?" he asked. "How can I make this decision as I am bound and also honor you?"

After a long wasting illness, Marie gave in to the dark rider, a smile on her thin, pale lips as she left the shadowed world of the weak and joined the bright world of the enlightened. Her last words to her husband were to follow his heart.

Since that icy night, he had aged a hundred years in one. The three parchments now weighted by golden trinkets on his giant desk had become his obsession as he tried to decide the future of his country, his kingdom and his two sons. He couldn't wait to die, to take his final breath and let the world do what it must. Sometimes he fantasized as he fell into his transitory sleep that he would not wake and the world would be left to figure its future without him. But his attendant roused him each morning, apologizing, bowing, averting his eyes as he handed his majesty a freshly cleaned robe and the same steaming bowl of the finest teas he had given his king since that first morning nearly fifty years past.

First he squinted at the will of his love, Marie. The will was a simple document, one scroll, written in her hand and attested by her life-long attendant, who claimed her maiden as sound of mind. The first paragraph regarded her worldly possessions, her crown, the tiara she wore as a princess of another land, the dress of her wedding day, the ring of her binding marriage to the king and a small wooden box given to her by a pheasant girl some years back, a girl who made it with her own hands out of love for her queen. She had no daughter, no niece and no sister and she gave these items back to her kingdom and her husband, the king.

The second and final provision regarded her authority and queenly power, which was nearly as vast as the king's. Normally this part of the document was a technical matter as the woman, if she were to die first, would always give to her mate her powers over the kingdom. She did this as custom demanded. But a sentence after the decree set the king's world askew.

This is what she wrote:

"These powers will be my husband's and my love's until his grieved passing. On that day, I hereby bequeath all the powers given to me as queen of the kingdom of Quell to his first son, a good man who will be a fair and noble leader. This be the last wish of my life."

As he read those words, his eyes red with tears and grief, he moved his attention to the official decree, a giant document containing all the rules and ordinances that directed the king and queen in the governance of their land. One of the parchments in particular had been his focus all these months.

Towards the bottom of the page one sentence sat alone:

"A bastard son is no son and will not rule this land."

Finally he looked upon his wife's letter. She wrote it in the last days.

This is what it said:

"My dear husband. You know as well as I the darkness of our son's soul. Even though we both be gone, I beg of you not to leave this land I have loved all these years in his rule. You know the man who should be king. I have forgiven your weakness those many years ago. Follow your heart, my love."

His first son was the product of an infidelity during the first months of his union to Marie. He loved the woman, the peasant girl, since he was little more than a child, though he knew they could never marry. He came to her one night shortly after his wedding to say farewell, or so he told himself. What he really wanted was to have her one last time, to love her and memorize all of her completely to last the rest of his life.

That final, desperate night produced a child, his first son, a bastard who by law was no son at all.

He confessed to Marie after three months of mental torture. They didn't speak for an entire year. But as time has wont to do, the sharp hurt in Marie faded to a dull ache and then finally, as it became part of who she was, to no pain at all, but rather a vague emotion that didn't feel like it was ever a part of her life. Their relationship healed and eventually they joined to produce a son of their own.

The door to his study rattled with an insistent knock, bringing the king from the thoughts that had consumed his will to live.

"Yes, enter," he coughed.

Two men entered the study, one with purpose and one with subservience. The second was the king's attendant, a man who had saw to the king's needs for all of his adult life, an old man himself now, head bald as a snowcapped mountain, back bent with the burden of diplomacy and eyes shrouded with dark rings of worry over his master.

The first was a young boy, in his twenties, dressed in silk and velvet imported from over the distant seas and produced by the finest slave tailors in all the world. He carried a wand with him. The king tried to tell himself it was a walking stick. But he knew it was a magical device, as black as the spells it aided. His hair was raven and slick, but his eyes were as green as a hillside during the first days of spring. His eyes appeared kind, as they were the same as his mother's, the same eyes the king loved nearly his whole life. But his mouth was twisted in a grim smile of arrogance and condescension, sarcasm and dark irony.

The attendant carried a tray with two bowls of the king's tea.

He placed them on the giant desk and looked lovingly at his king and friend.

The king nodded and his attendant took the three parchments from his desk, rolling two of them in reverence. The third he crumpled quickly in his hands and threw it in the crackling fire. He then backed out of the room leaving the king and prince to each other.

The prince sat across from his father and stared at him.

"Drink with me son," he said and reached for his own steaming bowl, a simple cup of finger-molded clay fired without pretense or design.

"No," the prince said. "I prefer more spirit in my drink."

The king sighed and shook his head.

"I'm dying, son. I might be gone by morning. Grant your old father a last wish and sip some warm tea with him."

The son nodded.

"With a promise such as that, how can I refuse?" He reached across the table and snatched his father's cup quickly away. "And I insist, then, that we drink together." He pushed his own tea across the table roughly, spilling some of it on the dark surface.

The king hesitated just a breath before accepting the drink. The prince watched him closely as the king brought the hot liquid to his lips, following suit just after his father. They both drank deeply, completely, and set the bowls down again.

"I intend to honor your mother's wishes," the king said. "You are not to rule this land."

The young man laughed. "You cannot stop me."

"I already have, my son." The king stood up, suddenly strong and steady. "The poison in your tea will be quick and painless. My last mercy to you, you who deserves no mercy."

"But I drank your tea," he said, whining. "I am smarter than you."

The old king laughed.

"Then you would have realized I stopped living the day your mother passed from this world. We are both poisoned and we will both soon be dead. And your half-brother will rule."

"They will never accept it. There must be an antidote. You cannot have killed me!"

"They will accept, my evil son. There will be no one else and the decree regarding bastard children now burns in that fire, there. Now, if you don't mind, I'd like to be alone." He walked around his giant desk and slipped from the library, leaving the prince in stunned silence.

The attendant found the old king's body the next morning, fifty paces from the library door, crumpled under a painting of his dear Marie.

CHAPTER TWENTY-SIX – HEALTH CARE

Time is suddenly growing short on this little book. The chapters are nearly complete. Where did the month go? How did these stories happen? I'm suddenly melancholy about the whole project, suddenly sad about my father and my mother all over again. Losing one was tough. Losing both was completely uncalled for.

My father died when I was nineteen years old, which spawned several years of chaos for me personally, several years of living someone else's life, of remembering my past as a dream. Now I look on those years between nineteen and maybe twenty-five and they seem like the fantasy.

The end of his life happened quickly.

One moment I had my father there, living at home, still working for God's sake, still managing his sales force by phone as they sped up and down I-5. I was going to college, albeit community college, but it was better than nothing at all. I was just beginning to refigure my future, to redistribute my hopes and dreams after realizing that engineering computers was not going to fuel the rest of my life. I was young and indestructible, totaling two vehicles within six months, just a little extra worry for my newly ailing father. I was selfish and superior and busy with my own endeavors.

The next moment my father, who had been in his bed a lot the last few weeks, was going to die. This was very inconvenient for me. What was he thinking? Okay, I know he was sick, but you'd think he could have put it off for a few more years. These were my years. How dare he screw them up? I didn't think that, of course, but the way I treated him over the last three months of his life I might as well have.

I continued going to the community college, continued dating the girl

I had met, continued to party and carouse and work my two jobs and be completely self absorbed with what was happening with me.

I know I had some conversations with my father. I vaguely remember sitting by his bed, watching him thin, almost before my eyes. I wish I had written it all down because I cannot remember any of it now. What did he say to me? What final wisdom did he grant me that I cannot recall? Certainly something in there would have made this journey easier. Certainly there was an old saying or a phrase or a story he shared with me in that dark, stuffy room that smelled like vitamins and bad breath that could have brought me to a better place. Or maybe not. Maybe he just asked me how things were and I asked him how he was and we both lied a little to each other out of selfishness and love.

When I think of it now, play it out, I feel the worst for my brother. I think he was fourteen at the time. I can't imagine his pain, and I can't forgive myself for not helping him. He's still such a sweet boy.

The day he died has a distinct, exact place in my cluttered mind.

I was at the college cafeteria, the quad, with my friends, laughing and joking about nothing in particular. I knew my father was close to his end day, but continued to go to school.

My girlfriend showed up, which was strange because she didn't have class that day. She called to me and I felt my heart shake in my chest. I knew from her voice and her expression what was happening.

"You need to get home," she said when I was close enough. "It's your dad."

I lived exactly fifty-three miles of winding, country road from the college. I don't exactly remember the drive, but I do know I was home in less than forty minutes. Wouldn't it have been the ultimate tragedy for a family to lose not just one mother, not just two mothers, not just two mothers and a father, but a sibling as well? I think I mentioned something about my own selfishness at nineteen?

My father, who sister number two had nursed in his own bed through his three months of illness, had fallen into a coma and was breathing heavily, raggedly, his body little more than a skeleton. Five of the six children were around him. Sister number one was frantically driving from her home, many more miles to cover the my measly fifty three. I'm sure there were others there as well. At least I think there were. I can't really say. I found a place to sit and we watched him take his last breaths.

I wasn't ready for the pain of his loss.

In the middle of one of his labored breaths he opened his eyes and looked at sister number two as if to say, "Here I go sweetie." And then he was gone, his body gone still, the constant noise of the last hour or so of his breathing gone, forever gone.

I didn't cry for my mother at the age of five with the shock of her sudden death. Maybe I was too young to understand it and then when I did understand the pain was too dull to cause tears. But I cried for my father, I cried hard. And when my first sister got there, not long after his last breath, I cried again.

I remember his funeral, or parts of it. I remember we sat in a section off from the rest of the visitors. I remember a lot of people were there. I remember someone, not me, reading a poem I had written for him. It was a birthday present for him from a couple of birthday's past and they read it over a microphone and I thought it sounded childish and stupid. I remember they put him in the ground next to my mother in a cemetery that sat not a hundred yards from my old grammar school.

And then my life gets a little fuzzy.

When I add up the years, I realize my father would be in his eighties today and I ask myself how long I expected him to live. The answer is always the same, "Long enough to see his grandchildren. Long enough to die not worried that his son was a mess fated to self-destruction and stupid mistakes. Long enough to be proud of the life I've made for myself."

If he had gone to see a doctor on a regular basis, he might still be around. If he had an annual check up, if the cancer hadn't spread up through his colon and into the rest of his body by the time he sought a physician, he may have been granted a few more years. If he had eaten a vegetable once in a while that wasn't out of a can, or a piece of fruit that wasn't part of a fruit cocktail. If ninety percent of his dinners hadn't begun with the words, "Steak and..."

But I'm being selfish here, and I know it.

My father was a tired, tired man. He had survived a war, a lifetime of chronic back pain, alcoholism, the death of his twin girls, the death of his first wife and the death of his second wife. He was ready to go, I think.

I wanted him around for two reasons.

One, so I could have him there, my security, my rock, as I stumbled into adulthood.

And two, so I could avoid the guilt for my seeming obsession with ignoring him and writing him off all those years, so I could have a chance to change my ways with him.

Both selfish reasons.

If he had just gone to the doctor.

CHAPTER TWENTY-SEVEN – BECOMING DAD

Right now, as I'm writing this, two of my four children are sitting under the kitchen table where I'm typing, pretending they are beavers. They are whispering because I just yelled at them and told them I couldn't think. Why don't they go in the other room? We have a big enough house. They have dozens of places to play. And yet they are at my feet, as if just me being close to them makes their adventure more fun. Even when I am shushing them.

My youngest daughter just looked up from under the table and said, "Hey Dad, how is it with your story?"

I told her I was almost done and she said that was great.

I don't deserve her. I don't deserve any of them.

My oldest daughter, the one who has been with me through all of it, has endured the learning-as-he-goes dad, is a shocking powerhouse of accomplishment.

In many ways I'm still that confused nineteen-year-old kid who doesn't know what he wants to do with his life and is unwilling to face anything more serious than a skinned knee.

It doesn't matter though, because here I am and there they are and for better or worse (no divorcing your parents) I have become their dad.

My dad was far from perfect. He made bad choices, suffered addictions, was gone a lot and avoided confrontations with his children. But there was something about him that made an incredible father.

How does a man become a dad?

Does he tell enough stories to his children that they grow up and tell their children? Does he have just enough sayings to make his kids think he's wise? Does he teach them how to ride their bike or drive a car or tie their shoes? Does he show them tricks to remember their right from their left? Does he protect them from the bad guys of the world and read them stories before bed? Does he check for the boogieman in the closet? Does he hang the outside Christmas lights at the end of every November? Does he make paper airplanes and pee in the snow? Is he bigger than life, Superman strong, and not afraid of anything?

I don't know if we can find an answer where we all say, "Oh, yeah, that's it."

I gave my father a kiss good night, right on the lips, until he died. How weird is that? I sat in his lap and watched TV with him until I was too big to fit with him in his chair. He told me he loved me every day. My father's name, Howard, means keeper of the home. And he kept our home, more than anything else, by simply loving us.

He loved me.

He LOVED me!

Dads aren't perfect.

They just love their children.

Can it possibly be that simple?

It was for me. That is what made my dad, my Dad.

When it comes to the practical side of raising kids - how to talk to them, discipline them, teach them, raise them - what little I know I didn't really learn from my dad. He gave me the genetic capacity to be a good father, the right kind of clay to be molded into a useful parent. But I had four older sisters with kids of their own to press the clay into a decent, kid-raising sculpture. I had four excellent examples of what a parent should do. I don't always do it. But watching them be fantastic mothers to their children for all of my life has been an education that can't be bought.

My kids are still sitting under the table at my feet. My son just said, "Dad, are you doing fine up there?" I don't think they are beavers anymore. They have turned the underside of the table into an office complex and they are working on some very important items of business.

I love them so much.

Appendix

    I want to share my father's recipe for Howie's Goodies from Chapter 5. As I mentioned, sister number four put this in a book with all of his other creations and variations. But this stands as the quintessential delicious and whether or not a person enjoys the odd combination of simple foods is often an indication as to whether or not they get to be in the family. Some of the children don't love it, but I think their taste buds are a bit underdeveloped, so we let them stick around. What follows is exactly how she wrote it down:

HOWIE'S GOODIES

    Ingredients:
    1 loaf soft crust French bread
    1 large package sliced salami
    4 large dill pickles
    2 cans chopped olives
    2 cups grated cheddar cheese
    2 cups grated Monterey Jack cheese

Slice French bread lengthwise to open face. Spread butter and garlic mixture on both halves. Spread one can olives on each half. Place salami slices over olives, making sure loaf is covered. Place thinly sliced dill pickle on an angle over salami. Sprinkle with cheeses. Place on cookie sheet and bake at 250 degrees until cheese melts and bread is warm.